John F Plimmer's

The Man who avenged Nelson

A tale of seafaring battles

'If I had been censured every time I have run my ship, or fleets under my command, into great danger, I should have long ago been out of the Service and never in the House of Peers.'
Horatio Nelson March 1805.

Introduction

Following the death of Vice Admiral Horatio Nelson, there were several Trafalgar veterans who later claimed to have brought down the French musketeer who killed England's favourite son. And yet, only one was credited with having avenged the death, which shook the whole of Britain. His name was John Pollard, an 18-year old midshipman serving on HMS Victory, Nelson's famous flagship.

According to a number of accounts given at the time, Pollard and another midshipman, Francis Collingwood, were on Victory's poop deck when they saw two enemy snipers, one of whom had fired the fatal shot, up in the rigging of the French warship, Redoutable. Both musketeers were killed by the midshipmen.

Sir William Beatty, the ship's surgeon wrote in the December 1805 edition of the Gibraltar Chronicle, that there were two men in the mizzen-top of the enemy ship, one of whom was killed by a musket-ball, and the other by Pollard.

Later, in an 1863 letter to The Times, John Pollard stated that Midshipman Collingwood had left the poop deck prior to the death of the French sniper.

Pollard was later taken before Sir Thomas Hardy and congratulated as having been the man to avenge Nelson's death. He was promoted in 1806 to the rank of lieutenant and continued to serve in the Royal Navy.

Little is known about Pollard's life prior to having served on HMS Victory as a Signal Midshipman. The account of his younger years is therefore fiction, much of that part of the book being supported by historical facts.

Those details surrounding the life of Horatio Nelson are indeed the result of research and are mostly empirically true.

The claim that John Pollard was the man who avenged Nelson has stood the test of time and no other individual was ever credited with such a feat.

The man who avenged Nelson, is therefore, prior to the Battle of Trafalgar, a dramatic account of what might have been.

Chapter One

It was indeed, a rare occasion for a rain squall to breach the harbour at Plymouth, and yet, as if in goading provocation, the waves lifted the small launch up into the air, in similar fashion to a rag doll being tossed unmercifully by the north westerly. The experience of the helmsman was obvious. The old seadog glibly grinned to himself, as the vessel carrying three men and a young boy, continued to joust its way towards the open sea. In addition to the helmsman, two armed red coated marines stood at the stern, looking as miserable as those they were watching over, exposed to the heavy rain peppering their backs.

The boy, John Pollard, was the only individual scanning the horizon with enthusiastic eyes. He had enlisted, whereas two of his three future shipmates had been forcibly taken off the streets by a press gang, and the third having accepted the King's shilling as an alternative to spending time in a debtor's prison.

Master Pollard had nurtured a burning desire to go to sea for as long as he could remember; the twelve-year old, whose blue top and white trousers were covered by a tarpaulin sheet, looked on excitably at the first sighting of his future home, HMS Havik. She was a war sloop remaining close to Plymouth's harbour, and rocking to and fro in the grip of the same adverse weather conditions coming up the channel; rhythmically rising and falling against her anchorage to the white flags tantalising both her bow and stern.

Captain Philip Bartholomew stood with his First Lieutenant, Basil Soames, on the quarter deck; both officers protected by sou'westers but with water dripping from their chins. The ceiling of dark clouds above their heads encouraged both men to think of warmer and dryer climates, yet it was not the junior ranking officer's place to enquire with his captain, when they would be sailing and leaving Britain's inhospitable elements behind. Or in fact, Havik's next location following orders from the Admiralty.

"New crew members sir," Soames remarked, as the captain raised his telescope to take a closer look at the launch bobbing up and down like a cork on the surface, drawing closer by the minute. He could see the occupants clearly and instantly realised, which of them were pressed men from the expressions on their faces.

One of the Royal Navy's smallest warships had recently seized and escorted the Swedish brig, Aurora of Gothenburg into Plymouth, after intercepting and seizing the vessel whilst sailing from Tenerife to Hamburg. The Aurora's cargo had consisted of several species of Barilla; salt-tolerant plants being the primary source of soda ash, to be later known as sodium carbonate. The result of the undefended action had been a share in prize money for each of the Havik's crew from the Admiralty's sale of the taken ship and its cargo.

"I take it they are pressed men Mr. Soames," the captain commented, taking note of the armed marines with rifles strapped to their shoulders.

"Two pressed, one a volunteer sir, and the boy enlisted."

"Very well, ensure they are escorted to their berths as soon as they come on board." Captain Bartholomew then retreated to his cabin for some respite from the severe wind and torrential rain.

"There ye be gents," the old sea dog said, bringing the small launch to the side of the sloop, "There's your home for the next few years, that's if Boney doesn't send you into the deep first." His words were accompanied by a cackling sound, which raised the eyebrows of the others.

All four new recruits climbed up to the lee gangway with the armed marines following closely behind. Soaked to the skin, they were met by the Second Lieutenant, a gentleman by the name of James Harkness, who wasted little time instructing a midshipman to escort the new crew members below. It was all adventurous stuff for the young Pollard, who couldn't resist grinning like a Cheshire cat, as the small group gained some respite from the rain. The lad's excitement soon subsided however, when he was first faced with the tiny, cramped conditions below decks. This was to be their berth for the foreseeable future and beyond, and two of the three men groaned when introduced to the dingy, poorly lit conditions. The hanging hammocks allocated to each of them, were certainly uninviting, and although they had all experienced a life of squalor beforehand, none had ever had to face such indigence as what was now presented to them.

"Don't be looking so keen youngster," the volunteer debtor quietly advised the ship's new cabin boy, "Thems in charge will only work you harder, take it from me. The more miserable you look, the less chance there be of getting yourself picked on."

"I've joined to serve both King and country," the boy naively answered, bringing a smirk to the older man's face.

"Well don't say I didn't warn you lad. By the way, my name's McCreadie, James McCreadie; Jimmy to my mates."

"John Pollard from Plymouth. Have you served before Mr. McCreadie?"

"You could say that. I've wet my whistle on a few of His Majesty's frigates, and don't call me mister. It's either Jimmy or Jock, or whatever name you want to choose, but never, mister."

The young lad nodded, having already worked out that his new acquaintance would be forever working hard to avoid whatever duties were bestowed upon him. Perhaps all the crew were of a similar ilk.

It was Midshipman Smiley who took the youngest member of the crew to one side, once the lad had deposited his kit bag on a swinging hammock strung up between two wooden posts, above another.

After introducing himself, the officer, who didn't appear to be much older than John Pollard, described the duties of the new cabin boy.

"Most of the time aboard, you will be required to carry messages to the captain and other senior officers," he explained, "And that might mean you having to run from one end of the ship to the other, so the quicker you learn the layout of the upper decks the better."

"Yes sir," Pollard answered.

"How's your stomach, Master Pollard?"

"Sir?"

"Sea sickness, how are you feeling? I detect some green in your cheeks."

"I feel fine sir."

"Very well, and in the King's navy we say, 'aye, aye sir', even when being addressed by the captain."

"Aye, aye sir."

From the nervous look on the youngster's face, Midshipman Smiley was reminded of his own first day on board, and understood the fear and apprehension his new charge would be feeling at that very moment.

"The quickest way to learn your duties is from your shipmates, and by carrying them out with all the enthusiasm you can muster, understand Master Pollard?"

"Aye, aye sir."

"If you need advice, then come to me. I am the first officer you will be accountable to as cabin boy. Any questions?"

"When will we be going out to sea, sir"

"Only the captain knows that, and only the captain will be aware of where we're going. Just one thing, the disciplinarian on this ship is the Boatswain, Mr. Swan. You'll get to know him soon enough, and when you do young man, do your very best to avoid him at all cost. He's extremely keen when using his rattan."

"What's that sir, if you don't mind me asking?"

Smiley chuckled to himself and answered by confirming, "It's a cane, and trust me you'll soon become acquainted with it, as soon as you give old Swannie the excuse to bind you across a cannon and lash your buttocks."

Pollard assumed it was the darkest side of life in the navy being described to him. But what if he was ever made to taste the lash without just course. From the tone of Midshipman Smiley's voice, no one would dare to challenge any action taken by the Boatswain. In fact, no seaman would ever dare to challenge any action of any officer whilst on board. The boy briefly recollected the time when his friend, Jimmy McNicholas was chased down one of Plymouth's narrow cobbled lanes by a greengrocer, from whom he'd just thieved a banana. Young Jimmy, an orphan who lived on the streets, easily outrun the overweight retailer, and confidently stood on top of a wall, bearing his backside to the man pursuing him. As the audacious lad confidently moonshined, the edge of a cane, held by a gentleman passer-by, cracked him harshly across his buttocks. Young McNicholas couldn't sit comfortably for a week after the event.

"Don't worry mister," Smiley continued, "Just keep your nose clean and work hard, and I'm sure you will be alright." The midshipman turned and left the new cabin boy to ponder on the advice shared with him.

Master Pollard's first duty was to access his hammock, and ignoring the few crewmen who were already in residence, began the daunting task of leaping up into the canvas cradle. Of course, initially he met with extreme difficulty, constantly falling back to the wooden floorboards, following each attempt. The more he failed, the more he became frustrated and blasphemed.

James McCreadie watched from a nearby berth, smiling to himself as the fiasco continued and beads of sweat began to appear on the boy's forehead.

"Wait," he finally called out, "Stand back lad, and watch me closely."

The older man then leapt off the floor with his back to the swinging hammock, landing in a sitting position, before lying back and enquiring, "Now then, do you think you can do that?"

After a couple more attempts, the young cabin boy was in situ, lying flat on his back and smiling at his own success.

McCreadie returned to his own hammock, shaking his head, and leaving the green recruit alone with his own personal and private thoughts. It wasn't surprising, that after just leaving home for the first time in his young life, Master Pollard's mind concentrated on the small terraced house where he had lived with his widowed father Thomas, and younger sister, Rose.

All of his life, he had desired to go to sea, seeking adventure and glory, and remembered the reoccurring dream he used to have when lying in the comfort of his bed with young Rose next to him. In his sleep he always imagined the same vision...

...It was one of the most influential sea battles of all time, resulting in the name of one British 100-gun flagship achieving infinity in her country's long history. The decks were littered with the bodies of injured and dying seamen and officers, lying side by side as the violence continued to erupt on every deck of HMS Victory. There standing proudly next to the Admiral was Midshipman Pollard, feeling no fear and assessing how the battle was progressing from the quarter deck of the British flagship.

"How goes the day, John?" Nelson enquired, turning towards his trusted friend and confidante.

"All is well sir," the lad answered, "The enemy is in retreat."

Suddenly, through the black smoke, Pollard saw a French musketeer, up high in the enemy ship's rigging, drawing a bead on Nelson who was standing next to him in his ceremonial uniform and medals. Instantaneously, in his dream, the young midshipman grasped a rifle. He had to move quickly, and managed to fire a lead ball into the chest of the sniper, watching as he fell to the deck of the enemy ship, as dead as a piece of timber.

"I am most grateful John," Nelson announced, in appreciation of his life having just been saved by the junior rank...

"John, John." The familiar voice called from far away, and he turned to look behind him, towards the poop deck at the stern of the ship, but his father wasn't there.

"Come on, boy. It's time to take out the cart."

The seven-year old lad woke from his dream, feeling somewhat exhilarated, having just saved Admiral Nelson's life. It was time to take the horse and cart out once again, to deliver bales of cloth to various customers in the sparsely populated neighbourhood, around Plymouth Sound.

John's father, Thomas Pollard, was a kindly draper, who managed to scrape a meagre living by selling various cloths to those who required them. His mother had died in child birth when bringing John's younger sister, Rose, into the world, leaving his father in the unenviable position of having to work hard to raise the two children in a life that was virtually governed by poverty. Almost each day, saw the tall, spindly gentleman with dark hair and side whiskers, always attired in the same black well-worn suit of clothing, struggle to keep sufficient food on the table for his offspring, and yet, he never failed.

Every morning on the fourth hour, the young feeble looking lad with the mop of unruly fair hair, helped his father with the round, returning home by about seven o'clock. One exception was when a special delivery had to be made to the Royal Navy dockyard at nearby Devonport. The navy was Thomas's most profitable customer, frequently requiring cloth for the manufacturing of uniforms. In most instances, when having to journey to the base, they wouldn't finish their round until approximately eight-o'clock, when it was time to wake John's sister, and prepare their meagre breakfasts.

Thomas's son always looked forward to his visits with his father to the naval base, and would often just stand there, admiring various warships in dry-dock for repairs or refitting. Whenever his domestic chores allowed, he would take Rose down to the harbour in Plymouth, and show her the commercial and naval ships moored there.

"One day, I shall go to sea, Rose," he once told his sister.

"Why?"

"Because, I feel the salt in my veins." John had read the same words, when being taught to read and write by his father, and had remembered them clearly, or so he thought.

"You mean you have salty blood John?"

"No silly. I yearn for the adventure of being on board one of those fighting sail ships I see each time I visit the dockyard with father."

"Can I come with you please?" she asked, her wide blue eyes staring up at her older brother.

"They don't allow ladies to join the navy Rose."

"But who am I going to play with when you've gone?"

He crouched down and kissed his sister on the cheek.

"Don't fret yourself Rose, it won't be for a few years yet."

Following his wife's unfortunate demise, Thomas found the small thatched cottage in which they lived, isolated, and with two young children to raise, felt the need for the company and support of closer neighbours. The small family moved to a terraced house in the town centre, close to an inn in which Mrs. Simpson, an old friend of his wife's, lived with her landlord husband. The same woman had been present with the local apothecary at the time of Rose's birth, and still took pity on the impoverished draper and his two young children.

John Pollard's fanatical enthusiasm for warships and battles at sea, remained with him in sleep, and his dreams were always of a similar pattern; Britain's most famous admiral's life would be saved. That was until on one occasion when his fantasy of glory disturbingly changed.

...The fear of Britain's population was evident. From the politicians in Westminster, to the workers in the fields, all hopes rested on this one battle at sea in which defeat wasn't an option to be considered. Only out and out victory would prevent the French Emperor, Napoleon Bonaparte, from extending his rule to include the throne of England. All along the coastline of France, armies of soldiers were waiting to cross the channel and invade the last country of resistance

to the dictator's ambitions. But first the Royal Navy had to be defeated by what the Marine Francais had to offer, and much depended on Midshipman Pollard's strategic ability to organise his fighting mariners.

The duel between the mighty warships began when Victory rammed the enemy's 74-gun flagship, the pride of the French Navy. Both powerful vessels became locked together in similar fashion to gladiators fighting in the arena, glued to one another in mortal combat. The rigging from both fighting ships seemed to be as one in the confusion, as the final drama was being enacted in the bid for supremacy of the seas.

Midshipman Pollard was taking everything in his stride, until at some point in the heat of the battle, he realised Admiral Nelson's flagship appeared to be doomed. French snipers continued to fire from above the bellowing clouds of smoke, bringing down those exposed on the decks below.

"We need to concentrate our fire on those musketeers up in the rigging sir," young Pollard suggested, but the Admiral just looked at him and smiled.

Utter carnage was surrounding each of Victory's severely damaged masts, as men in the King's service sacrificed their lives in efforts to be victorious. And yet, the pride of the Royal Navy continued to resist the determined enemy boarders with pistols and cutlasses, prepared to fight to the death and in reality, doing so.

Red coated marines and crewmen became entangled amongst the French onslaught beneath the blackened sky, as the will to fight on, remained hard fast and fervent. Former jailbirds and the pressed dregs of England's male population, fought like rabid dogs defending their territory from foreign invaders, as the noise of battle reached a new crescendo.

Midshipman Pollard appeared to be immune from the French onslaught and joined his shipmates at the stern, thrusting and slashing his cutlass at the enemy boarders. Then it happened. John glanced up, only to see the same musketeer from his earlier dreams, taking aim at the Admiral once again. A shot was fired, and in this visualisation, Nelson fell to the deck, mortally wounded...

John's dream, which was to be his last involving HMS Victory, turned out to be a nightmare, and he awoke with a start, covered in sweat.

Later that morning, when out on the cart with his father, he told Thomas of his strange mental perception, which had ended with the death of Horatio Nelson.

"Do you think it was a premonition father?" the boy asked.

"Nay lad, there's no such thing. You best forget all about it," Thomas advised, but realised just how determined his son's desire to go to sea had become. He hoped and prayed it was a mere passing phase, but much to the draper's disappointment, it quickly proved not to be the case.

As the years passed by, life for Thomas Pollard continued to remain a confrontation with hardship. The early morning deliveries continued, and he did his best to educate his son and daughter as best he could. Young John continued to excitably welcome visits to the naval dockyard, and a week never went by without the lad's inquisitive nature pouring out a stream of questions connected with the sea, and Britain's widely recognised domination of the waves.

Finally, in the same year as Napoleon ascended to First Consul of France, in 1799, the twelve-year old John Pollard applied to enlist in the Royal Navy, much to his father's distress. But Thomas knew that the sea had been like a magnet to his son since his earliest years, and could think of no way of stopping the boy from carrying out his wish. To do so would have been cruel and selfish. Of course, there would be one less mouth to feed, but the draper would have preferred to have continued his daily struggle with his son remaining close to him.

In November 1799, Britain's youngest naval recruit wrapped his arms around his sister, Rose, and kissed her on each cheek, instructing her to look after their father. He shook Thomas's hand and his father wished him well.

"Your mother would have been proud of you John," the elderly draper said, whose hair was by then beginning to show hints of grey, "And remember, there will always be a home for you back here."

"Thank you, father," the twelve-year old answered, "And please look after yourself." He might well have had the body of a child, but he'd been blessed with the mind and behaviour of an adult.

The boy turned away, to walk along the quayside, before joining a small group of other armed sailors and recruits in a launch, which would take them all to the ship. As it pulled away, Thomas and Rose waved their farewells with John's tearful younger sister blowing her sailor brother kisses. Although feeling self-conscious, he managed to wave back. In his mind he was a man now, about to serve King and country, and blowing kisses back to his younger sister went beyond the pail; or so he thought at the time.

Lying there in his hammock, listening to the sound of movement coming from the deck above his head, he took stock of events, which had occurred since coming on board. The youngster had been greeted by a totally different life to that which he had envisaged, and his first day spent on HMS Havik was to be filled with a mixture of wonderment and confusion. His first priority was, of course, to identify the Boatswain, Mr. Swann.

Chapter Two

The young Pollard believed his life thus far, when living at home with his father and sister had been congenial, thanks to the love and companionship the boy had shared under his father's roof. Now, having been inducted as a cabin boy in His Majesty's Royal Navy, the boy's domestic privileges had disappeared. His new calling was harsh and on occasions, even cruel, and the twelve-year old had to adapt far quicker to his new environment than he had ever anticipated. The youngster's dream of glory and adventure had not yet begun, but he strived hard to adapt, determined to fulfil all that he had hoped for.

Of course, Master Pollard's first few weeks on board Havik were always going to be difficult, and on occasions when disillusionment came visiting, he was greatly helped to shelve such emotion by the constant activity in which he immersed himself. All that his young eyes witnessed when on or below decks, was a new experience for him. Men appeared to be constantly running up and down the ship's rigging, trimming sails, reefing and securing them back in position, each accomplishment being timed by observing officers. Running the guns in and out was another daily chore, together with a thousand more duties necessary for maintaining a warship preparing to go to sea. A day rarely passed by without determined efforts being made to train the crew and improve on performances, no matter what the weather.

During his first couple of days on board, the youngster was left to explore the vessel, learning and noting the various component parts, including the binnacle in which the ship's compass was housed, close to the wheel. The wooden crate containing the various flags required to signal other ships, and located near to the main mast, was indicated to him. He watched closely as various stores were brought on board from the victualers on shore, including caskets of water, rice, beef in brine and other necessities, aimed at allowing the vessel to remain off shore for months to come. It was all so fascinating and educational for a lad who was yet to leave the waters of his home town, Plymouth.

Occasionally, Midshipman Smiley would enlighten his young charge on various aspects of life aboard one of His Majesty's ships. including whenever the captain would leave the ship in his brig and circle it from a short distance. Observed by Pollard and Smiley, the midshipman explained that Captain Bartholomew was only studying the way in which Havik was lying in the water, before returning and ordering the movement of items stored, to allow more efficient balance for when the ship would require to sail. In fact, Smiley proved to be a capable tutor, never ceasing to teach his young charge the basic rudiments of seamanship.

When facing the enemy, speed and accuracy would be of the utmost necessity, and the crew were rehearsed on a daily basis, until the First Lieutenant was satisfied with the progress made.

The new cabin boy invited his first admonishment, when being addressed by James Harkness, the Second Lieutenant. The officer was explaining some of the additional duties, which the youngster would be expected to carry out, at a time when John Pollard couldn't avoid averting his eyes towards all the activity ongoing around where they were standing.

"Look at me boy when I am addressing you," Lieutenant Harkness snapped, in an authoritative voice.

"Yes sir; sorry sir. I mean Aye, aye sir; sorry sir." He shuddered when he saw the Boatswain, Mr. Swann, glaring at him from the ship's bow.

"There is much to do young man and little time in which you have to learn what is required."

"Yes sir, I mean aye, aye sir," a bewildered cabin boy answered, knowing he had to focus more on detail, or risk the Boatswain's rattan.

"You will also salute all officers like this." Harkness touched the peak of his hat with closed knuckles.

"Aye, aye sir."

"Do your duty well boy, work hard, and try to avoid the bosun's birch, and I dare say we shall make a seaman of you yet."

"Aye, aye sir." How many times had young Pollard heard those words since first stepping on to the quarter deck? In fact, his initial fear of Mr. Swann had now developed into sheer terror.

The second lieutenant turned to Midshipman Smiley and instructed him to keep a closer eye on the youngest member of the crew, before dismissing both of them.

One of the least pleasing duties for the new cabin boy, was the carrying of bilge water from the bottom of the ship up through the lower decks, to be emptied into the sea. Apart from being physically demanding, especially for such a youngster who was still virtually a land lubber, Pollard hadn't yet quite got used to the stench below decks, each time he carried a bucket up for disposal.

The seamen's berth, in which he spent most of his leisure time with the other crew members, was dark and damp, oppressive and cold, and he wondered whether he would ever get used to such an environment of human indignity.

Midshipman Smiley described additional tasks to his young charge, confirming Pollard's life as a cabin boy would be a busy one.

"It is most important you assist the cook by carrying buckets of food from the galley to the forecastle, where your shipmates eat. You will therefore be required to report to the cook several times a shift to receive further orders."

"Aye, aye sir," the boy answered, still trying hard to come to terms with his new life.

The young midshipman smiled at the look of bewilderment in his young charge's, facial expression.

"There will also be occasions when you will be required to scramble up the rigging into the yards, whenever the sails have to be trimmed and of course, act as helmsman in good weather, to keep the ship steady on her course."

Those last instructions were unexpected, and the boy was beginning to doubt his abilities to succeed in his new career. Having watched others scupper up the rigging, he wasn't looking forward to having to follow in their footsteps.

"Please sir, how will I learn so much?" he nervously enquired.

"By watching your shipmates work, you will soon pick things up. But always remember..."

"To avoid the Boatswain."

"You're learning Master Pollard. Excellent."

"Aye, aye sir." The lad was beginning to sound like a parrot.

"One final word, keep yourself and your uniform clean at all times."

"Aye, aye sir."

In fact, in addition to carrying buckets of food to the crews' tables, Mister Smiley's charge was expected to dish it out on to the wooden dishes placed before them. On the very first occasion, with both arms resembling a sparrow's legs and exhausted from having just carried a bucket of salt beef broth for such a long distance from the galley, he placed his burden on top of one of the crochety tables.

"Come on boy," a fully bearded seaman demanded, "We're all starving to death here." The man looked as though he would need more than one plateful of broth to fill his oversized belly.

The lad had to summon all his strength to pull the ladle from the bucket, and when attempting to fill the seaman's dish, his hand began to violently shake, accidentally spilling some of the hot steaming grog into the other man's lap.

All hell was let loose, and the roar of surprise and anger could be heard throughout the lower decks. Without hesitation, the heavily built mariner stood from his bench and struck young Pollard across his face, sending him reeling to the wooden floorboards.

Pollard felt as if one side of his face had been removed, and the burning sensation resulted in a cry of immense pain.

"Now big man, why did you go and do that?" a voice enquired, "He's but a puppy, you overgrown fat turnip." It was James McCreadie, who was sitting at the same table.

"What's he to you?" the man asked, in a gruff voice with fire in his eyes, and trying to wipe the spilt broth off his grubby white trousers.

"Why, he's my younger brother see, you overweight jelly fish, which in my book gives me the right to represent his interests." McCreadie then quickly stepped around the table and dug his fist into the bigger man's mid-rift. He ducked under a swinging and powerful fist, before clubbing the aggressor to the floor by striking him on the back of his head with both fists clenched together.

Knives were drawn, and the other seamen cleared a space for the inevitable dispute, which threatened to result in one or both of the men cutting each other.

The bearded man slashed out with his blade, forcing McCreadie to leap backwards, before retaliating by kicking his opponent in the groin, forcing the bigger man back to the boards, gasping for breath.

"Belay that you men," a voice called out from close-by. It was Midshipman Smiley, appearing from out of the gloom, "What in Heaven's name is this all about?"

"No harm done sir," McCreadie answered, with a cheeky smile across his face, "We were just disagreeing about the name of the King's brother, and he slipped on some spilt broth."

Smiley turned to the cabin boy, who was still recovering on the floor; one side of his face flushed and swollen. The midshipman enquired if

Seaman McCreadie's version of events was true.

"Yes sir," John Pollard quietly, almost sheepishly lied, but saving his friend from at least a dozen lashes for having lied to an officer.

"Very well," Smiley answered, but obviously disbelieving what he had been told, "Clean this mess up and we shall say no more to the captain."

The one positive that resulted from the incident, was that the cabin boy's esteem greatly increased. Pollard was instantly recognised by the other crew members as a lad to sail the seven seas with, and was rewarded by their utmost respect. The youngster had proved, in the face of adversity, he was quite capable of supporting his ship mates. All except the bearded bully, who never spoke another word to Pollard or McCreadie, but was wise enough not to press home his complaint.

Life on board could have been even more difficult for young Pollard, had the ship been at sea. However, she remained at anchor for another two weeks, allowing him the opportunity to learn most things required to survive on Havik, in preparation for when the sloop finally abandoned the protection of the shore batteries. His only difficulty was being aware that both his father and sister were just half a mile or so on shore. No crew member was allowed to leave the ship, even when in harbour, from fear of desertion. He would often be found during his first few nights on board, staring across at the lights of Plymouth, trying to figure out which of them belonged to his family home. Of course, the youngster was feeling homesick, and could only hope such discomfort would leave him once Havik got underway to take him on his first voyage.

On one particular late evening, as John Pollard was staring down at the black sea below, and engrossed in past memories of his life ashore, a voice quietly came to him from behind.

"Penny for your thoughts young man."

He turned to see his newfound friend and protector, Jack McCreadie, standing there, smiling as he always did.

"I was only wondering when we shall be finally getting underway, Jack," the lad answered.

"Don't dwell too much on things like that young John," the mariner suggested, "Once we are at sea, youngster, the work will soon pick up and life for us all will become much harder, trust me."

The cabin boy couldn't think of anything to say in response to McCreadie's pearls of wisdom, and just nodded. It was obvious the former debtor had taken to the youngster, and was slowly earning his trust.

"The secret is never to rush things," McCreadie continued, "And always be aware of what is going on around you. Use what God gave you for brains, rather than what's in your heart my young shipmate."

"How can I do that Jack, when I don't know anything?"

"Experience my lad, feed your experience by using every hour to observe and watch without saying anything. Study how other mates behave and by copying their strengths you will condemn their weaknesses."

"Easier said than done, Jack."

"At first, but that's what experience is all about; learning from others until you have most of the answers locked up inside here." His friend tapped the side of his head with a finger.

Pollard genuinely appreciated the words of advice given so freely by Seaman McCreadie, and was thankful for his guidance and friendship.

Finally, and surprisingly, on the following day, John Pollard was sent for by the captain, and found himself standing outside Captain Bartholomew's cabin, where a red coated marine was posted, armed with a loaded rifle.

When instructed to enter the cabin by the captain's personal servant, a seaman by the name of Cruickshank, the youngster found the man in charge sitting behind a small desk. He was a heavily built man with a flushed face beneath a powdered wig. He had jowls which moved like a couple of jelly fish when he spoke.

"I see you are an enlistment young man?" the captain indicated, looking down at some papers resting on top of the desk.

"Yes sir," John nervously answered.

"Excellent, especially as most of the crew aboard are pressed men. So, tell me young Pollard, what encouraged you to join the Royal Navy?"

"I wanted to go to sea sir, and make a career for myself."

"Well said young man, but I fear you will find it hard work to begin with. I see from your personal docket; your father is a draper based in Plymouth."

"Yes sir."

"And I suspect you are already missing the comforts of home, am I correct?"

"No sir, I'm doing my best not to sir," John lied.

"Very well, then stay out of trouble and learn as much as you can about life on board, as quickly as you can, and I am confident you will achieve fulfilment."

"Yes sir, thank you sir."

"Then return to your duties and work hard young man."

"Yes sir, thank you sir."

After leaving the captain's cabin, young Pollard wondered what all of that had been about, apart from perhaps the captain was obliged to welcome every newcomer on board his ship. The boy assumed that's all it was, but at least Captain Bartholomew now knew him by name.

On the fifteenth night since the youngster had first stepped aboard, the sloop finally put to sea, with only the captain knowing the ship's destination. As Havik slowly maneuvered away from the sparkling lights of Plymouth, under full sail, the ship became a hive of activity, with crew members chasing up and down the rigging, attending to the sails. Orders were being relayed by the First Lieutenant, a tall, slim officer by the name of Basil Soames. A cannon boomed out from an on-shore battery, saluting Havik's departure, and one of the sloop's guns responded in kind. The captain stood proudly at the stern, giving verbal instructions to the helmsman, as John Pollard's home town slowly disappeared over the dark horizon.

Everything seemed to be so well organised, as a result of the many drills undertaken during the time the sloop had remained at anchor, and within a few minutes, the vessel had reached the open sea, making its way in the channel on a south by south east bearing, helped by a north westerly wind coming off the land.

"More speed if you please Mr. Soames," the captain ordered, "I'll have the reefs shaken out of the fore tops'l."

"Aye, aye sir."

As the Havik made her way down channel, the crew were left to guess whether they would soon be experiencing the warmer climate of the Americas or possibly the freezing conditions of the Baltic. It wasn't long before the answer became obvious. The sloop was to remain in the English Channel, joining with other ships to intervene foreign commercial vessels in British waters.

During the past two weeks in which men had been hurriedly trained to do their various duties, and efforts had been made to elevate the crew into some kind of acceptable coherent team of fighting men, the cabin boy had witnessed a number of disciplinary incidents. Most early mornings had been spent by every member on board, witnessing various punishments bestowed on individual miscreants, bringing home to John Pollard what navy discipline was all about. The twelve-year old had been made to watch two floggings and numerous lashings with the birch. Unknown to the lad, Jack McCreadie had always been standing nearby to support his young friend. But the cabin boy had taken the harsher side of life on board one of His Majesty's ships in his stride, often recalling the words of advice given him by the Second Lieutenant; not to solicit any trouble.

As the winter progressed and the snows returned, Pollard worked hard, obeying the orders given him, mostly by Midshipman Smiley, who often approached the youngest member of the crew with paternal understanding. Of course, there were the occasional errors, which went unpunished when there was no neglect or malice present. But it would only be a matter of time before, no matter how hard he tried to avoid the Boatswain's cane, John Pollard would fall foul of the ship's principle disciplinarian.

The cabin boy was directed by Lieutenant Harkness to secure the foremost Gallant sail, and in his haste to climb the rigging, felt his foot slip, before crashing back down to the deck. Luckily, he was not seriously injured, but lay on his back winded, with shipmates gathered around him, ensuring the lad was okay. Another crew member was given the same task allocated to John Pollard, and for the inconvenience resulting from his fall, the lad was dragged by one ear to the nearest cannon by the Boatswain, Mr. Swan, where he was ordered to prepare himself for punishment.

The subsequent experience was everything he had been dreading, and more. He felt each of the half dozen lashes bite into his exposed rear end, grimacing but refusing to cry out. When the callous punitive measures had been administered, the white cheeks of the lad's backside were covered in bloody stripes, and it was Jack McCreadie who carried him back down below decks to his hammock.

The experienced mariner made young Pollard lie on his stomach and eased the debilitating burning sensation by applying a balm to the wounds, telling his friend he would be given one hour before having to return back on deck. The beating was a harsh lesson learnt, but the result was a change in the cabin boy's attitude.

"One day Jack, I will give that bastard some of his own punishment," the youngster threatened.

"No, you won't," McCreadie chastised, "Take your punishment and leave it behind you Pollard. Otherwise your life won't be worth living." He then removed his own shirt and proudly displayed scars across his back, put there by the cat o nine tails.

"That's what I picked up when sailing on frigates, and believe me boy, when I tells yer, once you taste the cat, it makes you more wary and you never wants to be caught out agin. There's no place on board any ship for holding grudges." It was yet another lesson well learned.

Many days and nights passed by, as Havik patrolled the English Channel, before the cabin boy's discomfort left him and he was capable of using a stool again. During that period, Jack McCreadie paid the lad special attention, often lecturing him when an opportunity presented itself. Young Pollard gained a great deal of inspiration from much of the advice shared by his older shipmate, who seemed to have a way with words. On one occasion, a philosophical lesson was given on the way in which a ship at sea was like a floating island.

"We are the only inhabitants on the island, and everything is shared amongst us, including duties, meals, places to get our heads down, moments of peace and quiet, and moments of terror, believe me son."

"Aye, aye sir."

"And you never call a shipmate, 'sir'. That's reserved for them that gives us orders." McCreadie demanded, "On board ship, we're all an isolated gathering of men. It's a way of life with rules of conduct and social order. You'll soon discover, when at sea your very survival depends on doing your work well, from navigating to hauling on a line; not for the King or the captain and his officers mind you, but for your shipmates."

Although John Pollard hadn't received the kind of education that most of the officers on the Havik had been fortunate enough to have been privileged to, he was quick to pick up, what was to him, a new language. The basic descriptions of various parts of the ship were already known to him, such as the front was referred to as the bow, and the back, the stern. Other less known references included the Bowsprit, a spar used to hold jibs at the bow; the Keel was the backbone of the vessel, running from the bow to the stern. A mast wasn't as he had thought, just a sail, but a large wooden spar set in the decks and used to hold up other spars and the rigging, including the foremast at the bow, the main mast in the middle and the mizzen mast at the stern.

The cabin boy was surprised at the number of different sails required to maneuver a ship; jibs were triangular sails at the front of the ship and attached to the bowsprit. Square sails varied from the main sails, which are the lowest, the topsails being the next highest and the topgallant sails at the very tops of the masts. Above those are the royal sails. One other new name to Pollard was the 'Spanker' – the biggest sail at the stern of the ship. It was all new to the youngster, and he often lay in his hammock trying to remember the various names, but as the majority were mentioned on a daily basis, he quickly became accustomed to the new language.

One other aspect of life at sea was the manner in which seamen spent their leisure time when not working or sleeping. Traditionally, the majority were hard-drinking and toughened individuals who had no other option but to make the best of their cramped living quarters. But whenever an opportunity came their way, they practiced tying knots, sketching, carving, model making and playing games of cards or dice. Communal or solo singing of old sea shanties was another popular pastime. It seemed that everyone took pleasure from crying sentimentally from the words and melodies that would take over the lower decks, usually to the accompaniment of a mouth organ or whistle.

What was missing for the twelve-year old John Pollard though, was action, for which he yearned. It was three months of laboriously patrolling the channel, before it finally came...

Chapter Three

On the evening of the 29th January 1800, a call for 'All Hands' echoed throughout the sloop, as she cruised just southward of the Scilly Isles. A grey murky dusk was descending upon the waves, and a sensation of unexpected excitement ran through the Havik, as men suddenly appeared from nowhere.

"You, master-at-arms, take the name of the last man up through the hatch." It was the voice of the captain, and within seconds every member of the crew was at their posts in readiness for the next order.

There was a stiff channel westerly breeze and it was necessary to trim the sails, to lie as close as possible to the wind. Orders were given and individuals were soon chasing up the rigging, like men born to carry out such feats of daring. Then came the order the ships company had been waiting for.

"Set courses and top gallants Mr. Soames and clear for action," the captain directed the First Lieutenant, "But belay running out the guns, if you please."

"Aye, aye sir, clear for action and belay running out the guns," Captain Bartholomew's second in command replied. It was customary on a ship of war to repeat every order given, to ensure clarity before execution.

Master Pollard felt like a lost soul amongst the ongoing melee. Was this to be his first action; that which he had yearned for being involved in for as long as he could remember? The youngster was desperate to find out, and looked in earnest for Midshipman Smiley. He found his mentor standing on the quarter deck, barking out orders, and watched with enthusiastic eyes, as barrels filled with parchment cartridges of gunpowder were quickly brought up on deck from below, before being placed at the side of each cannon. The gunners were supplied with slow burning match and buckets of water were positioned at strategic points, in readiness should fire suddenly break out. Every crew tasked with handling the ships munitions, did so in bare feet or rubber soles to prevent the slightest spark, which threatened disastrous results.

"Sand Mister Smiley," the First Lieutenant loudly directed, prompting the junior rank to detail a small group with the responsibility of covering all decks, to avoid men slipping on the wooden boards.

Then the response, "Cleared for action sir," confirmed the Havik was ready to engage any enemy, as the captain and other officers stood near to the stern rail of the ship, each looking northwards towards the horizon.

Smiley turned to the cabin boy and told him to quickly take a message to the captain, enquiring what ammunition was to be used for the cannons.

"What kind of ship are we going to fight sir?" Pollard asked, remaining in awe of what was going on around him.

The midshipman smiled back at him, and in a low voice explained, "Use your eyes Pollard. See over there on our port side."

The youngster stared across at three British warships, which were part of the same group as the Havik.

"Yes sir," he answered, still confused.

"One of them, Suffisante, has signalled for us to engage a cutter heading north. They have two other vessels in their sights, which are trespassing in our waters. Now go and deliver that message boy, and be quick about it."

"Aye, aye sir."

The cabin boy went scurrying off, racing towards the ship's stern. The Boatswain, Mr. Swann, could be seen standing on the quarter deck, bawling out orders to various members of the crew, with his notorious cane grasped in one hand. Pollard purposefully avoided the officer, as he made his way aft. When he reached the stern, he stood just a few feet from the officers gathered there.

"There she is sir," the second lieutenant, James Harkness could be heard to say, "On the starboard bow."

All eyes were raised to telescopes, and pointed in the direction of a vague shape in the distance.

"She's running low in the water sir," Lieutenant Soames observed.

"Aye mister, that she is," the captain answered, "Hands to the sheets Mr. Harkness, jibe her over."

The order was instantly obeyed, and very quickly the wind filled the Havik's top masts.

"Heavy cargo and a pretty prize indeed Mr. Soames," The captain suggested to his First Lieutenant, who then turned and saw John Pollard standing there.

"What is it boy?"

"Please sir, Mr. Smiley is asking what ammunition should we use in the guns, sir." The cabin boy wasn't sure whether he should touch his forehead in way of saluting the most powerful man on the ship, and did so rather than risk his wrath.

"Not much I fancy, by the look of her," the captain answered, turning back to view once more his target. There was a pause in conversation, as Captain Bartholomew thought out his decision.

"Link shot boy," he finally instructed, "We don't want to sink her. Tell Mr. Smiley to inform the gunner we shall use link shot on five cannons and to have the remainder loaded with nine pounders."

"Aye, aye sir."

Pollard couldn't get back to the midshipman fast enough to deliver the reply to his message, and then stood back and watched as the order was given. A quantity of long chain links was loaded into each of five of the cannons, and for the first time, the cabin boy watched and learned as the remaining fifteen big guns were loaded with nine-pounders. Such maneuvers were more involved than the youngster had imagined. Firstly, each gun was pierced by a metal pricker through the touch hole and fine grain gunpowder added. A cloth wad was then placed into the barrel before a powder cartridge quickly followed. The shot was next, before yet another wad to prevent the cannonball from rolling out of the barrel should the muzzle be depressed. Everything was rammed down tightly and the cannon was ready to be fired. After each shot was fired, a wet swab would be used to swamp out the barrel's interior to extinguish any hot embers, which might setoff the replacement charges of gunpowder prematurely.

It soon became clear that the use of link shot was intended to rake the decks of the opposing ship, targeting personnel in an attempt to disable the vessel. It was all mesmerising stuff for a twelve-year old boy, and before long the crew could see the ship they intended to attack quite clearly, heading towards them through the dusk. There appeared to be no attempt to move away from Havik.

The sloop changed tack, so as to approach the other broadside on, and James Harkness was in position on the gun deck, awaiting firing orders as the British ship approached what looked like, a commercial vessel. The name displayed on the cutter was 'The Strafford'.

An order for one shot to be fired across the cutter's bows was executed, resulting in the other ship coming immediately to a virtual standstill. The Strafford's captain could be seen holding a cone shaped instrument to his mouth, and he called to the Havik, enquiring as to the reason she had fired on his ship.

"Who are you and what is your destination?" Captain Bartholomew asked, also using a loudhailer.

"The Strafford from out of Baltimore, carrying tobacco to London. We were taken as a prize by those two other jackals captain." The man was obviously referring to the two privateers, Suffisante and the others had gone chasing after.

Havik's captain could see no reason for making any further enquiry, accepting the other skipper's explanation without hesitation.

"Very well. Be on your way sir."

It was an anti-climax, and John Pollard's first action had witnessed only one warning shot being fired. But at least he'd seen at first-hand how the ship prepared itself to attack a possible enemy. There was no doubt, the speedy and efficient manner in which she had been cleared for action, was the result of the training exercises back in Plymouth. Just as impressive was the quickness and manoeuvrability displayed by the sloop when bearing down on a possible enemy.

The two privateers that turned out to be the lugger; 'Courageux' and cutter; 'Grand Quinola', were captured by the group led by Suffisante and returned to Plymouth as prizes of the Royal Navy. The money obtained from the sale of both of those vessels would be shared amongst the crews of all ships within sight of their capture, which when it came down to a mere cabin boy serving on the Havik, was negligible.

During the months that followed, Havik returned to Plymouth on several occasions, escorting various pirate ships working in the English Channel. They included two French brigs and a Dutch East Indiaman. On the 28 February 1800 the Landrich became a prize to Havik when sailing from San Domingo for Bremen. Within a month of that incident, the sloop returned to Plymouth with the Landrake, carrying a cargo of sugar from San Domingo to Hamburg. Many others followed, and John Pollard became frustrated by being frequently anchored so near to his father and daughter on shore, each time Havik entered Plymouth harbour. But the order that none of the crew were allowed to leave the ship was reinstated, resulting from a long history of sailors getting drunk and deserting. Captain Bartholomew was taking no chances.

Although confined to the sloop whenever she came into port, the morale of the crew remained high. Capturing so many prizes and receiving their share of the spoils, was a satisfactory consolation and helped the men focus on their duties. None of them actually saw real action until September of the same year.

Both Havik and Suffisante encountered a French flotilla of fourteen vessels carrying provisions and supplies to the French fleet at Brest. The ships were being escorted by an 18-gun frigate; 18-gun corvette, and a brig with 14 guns. The British ships engaged the escort and a chase followed, with cannon fire coming from both sides of the engagement. During one episode, when the sloop encountered the French frigate at close range, she had her railings at the bow, shot away, killing one of the crew. That was Havik's first dead casualty of any confrontation, and in retaliation she managed to severely damage the Frenchman's main mast.

Eventually, as the two British warships began to turn the confrontation in their favour, the French managed to gain the protection of shore batteries near Morlaix. Both Havik and Suffisante were forced to retreat from the additional fire power. Two additional members of Havik's crew were severely injured during the chasing skirmish, including one of the officers, Lieutenant Bayley, who later died from his wounds. It was the first time the young cabin boy had witnessed the loss of lives, and experienced the first of many burials at sea, conducted by the captain. But the failure at attempting to capture some of the French convoy was a major disappointment to all on board Havik, although they were unaware at that time, a greater disaster was to follow.

Shortly after the unfortunate action at Morlaix, the sloop, having been tasked with patrolling the sea room between the Channel Islands and the

Ile de Batz, intended anchoring in St Aubyn's Bay, Jersey, for repairs and the transfer of wounded crew members to an onshore hospital. The captain had also received written orders from the Admiralty, to take on board a local pilot to assist with negotiating the coastline close to Ile de Batz.

All appeared to be going well, until, just prior to entering the harbour at St Aubyn's Bay, the sloop lost her anchor and the carpenter was called upon to make a temporary replacement in all haste.

Captain Bartholomew stood in his usual position near to the stern railing, with his First Lieutenant, Basil Soames; both officers watching with some concern at the black clouds approaching the Jersey coastline.

"Let's just hope the storm is not too severe sir," Soames remarked.

The wind was beginning to come up, as the vessel anchored just inside what little shelter the harbour offered. The skipper commented that he was concerned the makeshift anchor might not hold.

"God willing, it does," he remarked, but remained anxious, wishing the approaching storm had allowed for more time to see Havik safely anchored well inside the harbour.

But Lady Luck abandoned them, and as the dusk was falling rapidly, the winds increased in velocity. Then, as the surrounding greyness turned into the pitch of night, Havik lost her temporary anchor and the vessel began to move, heading inwards towards the shore.

The captain called to the helmsman, as the ship began to drift and waves began to break over the bow, flooding the upper deck at the front of the ship. It was quickly confirmed there was no bite in the rudder and that control of the vessel had been lost. More men were put to the pumps, as the water continued to fill Havik, but it was a hopeless task. The pumps were ineffective against the tidal wave of water gaining the upper decks, and it was only a matter of time before Havik failed to stay afloat.

Both the captain and his First Lieutenant could feel the sloop lowering in the water. Every seaman's worst nightmare was happening. She was sinking in what had developed into a fully blown storm, wreaking havoc on the upper decks.

As the howling wind played tunes in the rigging, all appeared to be lost, but efforts to save her had to continue through the driving rain, until the inevitable was confirmed. Orders were given for the crew to cut away her masts and pitch her guns overboard, in an attempt to make her lighter. Every member became involved in the tasks allocated, including the fearful cabin boy. It was a relentless fight for survival.

"I take it you can swim Jonno?" Jack McCreadie asked, as he frantically cut away rigging from the foremast with other members of the crew.

"No, I've never learned," the young lad answered.

"Then you best stay close to me boy. Having said that, the way she's heading, she might just ditch in shallow water."

The winds grew stronger and louder as they continued to blow the small sloop inshore, until finally the sound of her keel finding bottom, confirmed she was grounded on a sandbank with the lights of St Aubyn's visible in the distance. So near and yet so far away.

Other ships positioned in the bay, were subjected to the same ordeal, but managed to remain afloat. Lieutenant Soames suggested they could request one of the other vessels, namely the Pelican, to attempt to pull Havik off the sand bank, on which she was stuck, but if that was successful, the sloop would still be in the same position as before, without any helm control. It was a dire and hopeless position facing the captain.

For another six hours, the storm continued to batter the sides of the helpless vessel, with wave after wave flooding the lower decks, as the stricken vessel sat there, motionless and at the mercy of the elements.

"I believe we've lost her Mr. Soames," Captain Bartholomew finally confessed.

"Shall I order the crew to abandon ship sir?"

They were still some way off from the shore, and the captain shook his head, thoroughly dejected, like a man who had just been well beaten in a skirmish with the French, and with no escape available.

"No, Mr. Soames. We would lose too many men trying to reach the shore from here. If she can stay afloat until the tide turns, then we shall look at our position again."

Finally, as daybreak came, the tide, which had risen some thirty-two feet, receded; the winds dropped and the sky cleared as quickly as the storm had descended upon them during the night before.

"Use every boat and launch we have, Mr. Soames, and get these men off, wounded and non-swimmers first."

"Aye, aye sir."

John Pollard was one of the first to be taken in a launch to the safety of the shore, feeling totally confused by all that had happened. Having been a member of the Havik's crew for just a year, he had witnessed his first shipwreck, and now, like the rest of his shipmates, was without a berth. Fortunately, there were no casualties and the vessel was eventually abandoned, as a wreck.

After transferring what items of importance, including the ship's records, to HMS Pelican, the captain and crew were Also transferred to that vessel, for returning to Plymouth. Although life on board any naval vessel was hard for the crew members, no one wanted to see the ship they served on, come to such a dramatic end as that suffered by the Havik, and the Pelican left the Channel Islands with an extremely dejected and solemn crew from the abandoned sloop. They were similar to orphans who had just seen their orphanage burnt down, and all without striking a blow against the enemy. Nothing could be more demoralising.

As the British shoreline became visible, the now former cabin boy asked his closest friend, Jack McCreadie, if he was going to wait for another ship to serve on.

"There's no fat chance of that boy," the more experienced mariner quietly admitted, "As soon as we reach Plymouth, I'm heading back to Portsmouth and that's the last the navy will see of me. What about you youngster?"

"I'm going to try and get a berth on another ship, if it's possible, Jack."

"Oh, it'll be possible alright. If you don't volunteer, you'll soon get pressed into service. Once the navy has a record of your name, that's it. You are always one of the first they'll call on to man their ships, whether we're at war or otherwise. In England, the navy comes before anything else, and we're the prats who have to serve."

After a month following the demise of the Havik, John Pollard was returning to his family home, with what little belongings he had, stuffed inside a canvas bag he carried across his back. It was strange, as he walked through the narrow-cobbled streets of his home town, how much he found he was missing the sea already. Although, the youngster had adapted to the cramped conditions in the unfortunate sloop, he sensed a feeling of claustrophobia as he mingled through the crowded streets. The air he breathed wasn't as invigorating as what he had experienced at sea, and the absence of the intense activity and conversations ongoing at the same time, had a distinct effect on him.

There was no more singing, laughing, joking or altercations that were all part of life on board one of His Majesty's warships. Even before he reached the front door of his father's terraced house, he was homesick for the life he had just been compelled to abandon. And the men who had added so much richness to his everyday duties.

It was his sister, Rose, who answered the door, and immediately cried out his name, before throwing both arms around her brother's neck.

"Father's out, delivering some cloth over in Devonport," she quickly explained, "But look at you. You're home now John for good. Or will you be going back?"

"I don't know just yet Rosy, but my, how you have grown in the past year. Is there any food in the house, I'm starving?"

Chapter Four

John Pollard had never experienced such raw fear before that night, stranded off the Jersey coastline, and hoped and prayed he would never again see a ship upon which he served, lost in such a dramatic manner. At least, when sitting below decks in the future, listening to the stories and tales from other shipmates, he would now have one of his own to tell.

By the time their father arrived back home and stabled the horse, his son had devoured two plates of bread and cheese, a large glass of ale, and was in the middle of mesmorising Rose with numerous tales of his short time spent at sea, including his most recent traumatic experience. He was warmly welcomed by Thomas Pollard, who after eating the supper put before him by his daughter, sat opposite John, in the small parlour, listening intently to all the details of the disastrous fate of the Havik.

"Do you think Captain Bartholomew will be given another ship John, after losing his command in such a dreadful fashion?"

"I've no idea father, that's above and beyond me, but I did like the man immensely and can only wish him well in the future."

The truth of the matter was that the Admiralty looked harshly upon any captain that lost his ship in any circumstances, and it was highly unlikely Captain Bartholomew would ever be given a command again. In all probability, he would be retired on half pay.

"You were lucky to escape with the others John," Thomas remarked.

"Yes father, but we all managed to get away and were brought back to Plymouth in the Pelican."

"Thank the Lord for that. But what happens now? I mean, will the navy find you another berth?"

"I think so father, but Lieutenant Harkness told me I might have to wait some time before they recall me."

"I fear that won't be too long John. There's a French tyrant across the channel causing all kinds of mayhem and threatening to take over most of Europe. I shouldn't think it will be too long before Britain goes to war again. In the meantime, I can't compensate you with much coin, but would appreciate a helping hand with deliveries."

"I would love to help you father, for as long as you want me to."

"Or when the navy comes calling again?"

Surprisingly, the navy didn't call to serve enlistment papers on the former cabin boy, not for some time to come. During a two-year period following his return home, Master Pollard's life once again consisted of delivering cuts of cloth on his father's behalf. Every morning, he took the horse and cart out to neighbouring town houses, farm dwellings, church vestries, retailers and where ever there was a call for woven and spun bales. Rose often went with him on the early morning calls, leaving their home at four in the morning and returning in time to make breakfast. The extra pair of hands were appreciated by their father, who was finding it more difficult to move about, owing to bouts of severe lumbago and arthritis. His son's presence was a God send, and he often showed his pleasure at having young John back in the fold again.

In similar fashion to how the two siblings used to visit the harbour and look out towards the ships moored there, when children, John often took Rose to point out some of the warships, comparing them with the commercial vessels. His thirst for the sea never left him, and as the days, weeks and months went by, he began to fret that any future in the Royal Navy was beginning to look doubtful.

During his respite from the sea, John's voice broke, and his sister found it extremely humorous, when listening to the deep guttural sounds being projected whenever in conversation with her brother. He was quickly entering manhood, and began to feel frustrated at not being where he had hoped to be at such a time in his young life.

The seasons came and went, and eventually the dreams of yesteryear returned. But not of a glorious battle involving attempts on Nelson, but involving Captain Pollard risking his war sloop in battles with the French. It seemed that all people ever talked about was the subject of the Corsican tyrant across the channel, as news of French victories reached them more frequently than they desired. The map of Europe was drastically changing, and with rapidity, as Napoleon's armies marched on dominantly, fighting and conquering all in its path.

Most evenings were spent by the fireside in conversation with his father. They would discuss recent events, as reported in the newspapers and journals, including the antics of the French across the channel. Thomas Pollard noticed the underlying anguish in his son's voice, accepting that frustration was beginning to show, especially when mention of British warships lying idle offshore was reported in various printed circulations.

On one particular winter's evening, as all three of them sat in candle light, with Thomas reading from a day-old newspaper he had come by earlier, he explained to both his son and daughter that the First Consul of France, Napoleon Bonaparte, had inherited a chaotic republic. According to the same report, 'Boney' was the saviour of France.

"Aye, if this article is to be believed, it seems that over the past two or three years, he's managed to create a stable economy and strong bureaucracy. It could be propaganda though. You just don't know what to believe these days; there's so much confusion and uncertainty in the world."

"I heard though father, Napoleon's victories have been the result of a well-trained army, which is admired by the majority of the people he serves. Perhaps that's propaganda as well," John remarked.

"We shall just have to wait and see."

"If all was well in France, why would he need to expand his territories, strengthening his military with conscripts from those countries he's conquered?" John had also read suggestions that Napoleon often forced those members of defeated armies into his own lines.

"Land grabbing to a man like Boney, is like an intoxicant, that's why John. Mark my words, as things go, very soon England will be the only power left to defy him. Like all tyrants, he doesn't seem to be the kind of man who will ever be satisfied with what he's got. And as long as he's putting bread on the tables of his people, they will continue to support him."

"Do you think he will ever try to invade England father?"

"Eventually, I wouldn't be surprised, but that's where the Royal Navy will come into its own John. To invade us, he has to bring troops across the channel, and to do that he must first defeat the King's navy, and I can't see him having a cat in hell's chance of doing that. I'm surprised we haven't already started rebuilding our ships in readiness."

John remembered what his old shipmate, Jack McCreadie, had once told him, that a ship was like a floating island, and considered Britain to be similar, surrounded by water, as she was. His father's words were wise, and from his own experience of serving in the Havik, the young man was confident there was no other navy in the world that could defeat Britain's expertise at sea, supported by those magnificent ships of the line. And yet, he was aware that the majority of crews had been paid off and vessels had been left moored, like ghost ships not manned, in order to save money. He could only hope and pray that one day, he would serve on one of those awesome 74-gun vessels. Why was it that the politicians were reluctant to invest in the country's defence, until a major threat became a reality?

Whenever he could, he visited his mother's grave in the cemetery at nearby St Martins Church, where he would kneel and reiterate all his experiences when serving on the Havik. On another occasion he returned to the old thatched roof cottage where they had once lived, only to see it had been turned into a shed, and was being used as a feed store for cattle during the winter months. It was where he and Rose had been born, and he couldn't help but feel a wave of sentimental regret, as he walked through the now empty rooms, treading on hay and manure covering the ground floor. It was all so regretful and depressing, and his lust for the sea strengthened even more.

When he later mentioned what he'd seen to his father, Thomas just told him that, sadly, life had to go on and it would be folly to dwell too much on the past.

Almost two years had gone by, when John Pollard received that official letter he had been anticipating for so long, from the Admiralty. The navy had been restored back to life, and various defeated countries were desperate for help from Britain. Once again, the King had formally declared war on the French tyrant, and the former cabin boy was to report to HMS Culloden at Portsmouth. The real surprise was that he was to carry the rank of midshipman.

A wave of excitement swept through the draper's son, and he received the congratulations of his sister, and blessings from his father. Yet, all three of them realised that things would be much different now that John would be re-entering the service at a time when his country was at war with their neighbour across the channel.

"May the Lord be praised," his father announced with genuine pride, "You are to become an officer John. You surely must have made an impression when serving as a mere cabin boy on the Havik. I wonder, ignoring all the innuendo and suggestions made by the circulations, just how effective the French fleet is?"

"Not effective enough, father," John answered, confidently and wallowing in the thought of receiving the same entitlements as his old friend and mentor, Midshipman Smiley. At least now, having achieved officer rank, he would be given half pay should he be forced to leave the navy. The young man appreciated half of a midshipman's pay wasn't anything to celebrate, but it would still be better than nothing. Far better than having to become impoverished.

However, Thomas Pollard held much doubt and secretly worried for his son's safety, knowing his ship, Culloden, would surely be engaged in more than just the capture of commercial ships and prizes in the channel.

One advantage of being the son of a draper, was that John Pollard didn't have to purchase his own midshipman's uniform. His father made one for him. The garment consisted of the finest blue frock coat made from the best quality serge with a white button collar patch denoting his son's designated rank. He couldn't help but feel proud when first seeing it on John's back. The recently promoted midshipman looked smart and, although his childhood features had remained, he genuinely looked a Royal Naval officer. The only thing missing was the appropriate peaked hat, and Thomas escorted his son to Devonport, where the young Pollard was issued with the final item of uniform, which displayed the name of his ship across the front and above the shiny peak.

The time finally arrived when Midshipman Pollard had to leave home for the second time, his instructions being to travel to Portsmouth, to join his ship. Before stepping into the carriage, which would take him away, yet again, he kissed his tearful sister on both cheeks and hugged her closely to him.

"God speed my boy," his father said, shaking his son's hand, "And you will be in our thoughts every day you are away."

"Thank you, father, and both of you will be in mine."

Both father and daughter watched as John's transport disappeared in the distance, taking their son and brother to a war, which promised to be more perilous than any other previous confrontation.

"He will come back to us father, one day, won't he?" Rose asked, seeking reassurance.

"Of course, he will, Rose. Your brother is a young man now, who knows how to avoid danger. He'll come home, once this French tyrant has been defeated."

As he travelled through the beautiful and colourful scenery of Hampshire, John Pollard admired the cloudless blue sky and patchwork fields with green hedgerows lining the thoroughfares. For the briefest of moments, he wondered if he would ever see England again. And yet, bizarrely, he would swap all of his country's rural beauty for a grey sky and tempest at sea. But what if he was killed, or severely handicapped? What if the downside of war at sea caught up with him and his legs were violently swept away by a shot from an enemy cannon? The young man had to vanquish such dark thoughts from his mind. He sat back with both hands clasped behind his head, convincing himself that the oceans of the world were still in his blood. Eventually, he felt more at ease; more contented than he had been since leaving the Havik abandoned in the harbour at St Aubyn's Bay.

His thoughts began to concentrate on a thousand things awaiting his attention, once he'd embarked on HMS Culloden, the most disturbing challenge being how he would fare in his new rank. The fact, he was now a naval officer, had come as a shock, and it would be a long time before he actually came to terms with the Admiralty's decision.

Once he arrived at Portsmouth, he wasted little time in finding the launch moored at the quayside, in readiness to transport new crew members to the mother ship. Midshipman Pollard was further surprised when the sailor in charge of the launch, touched his cap in salute and addressed him as, 'sir'. Nervously, the young man from Plymouth responded, having to quickly recall what he had been taught about saluting when serving on Havick.

Two other recruits, each holding the same rank as John, were sitting in the launch, and all three nodded at each other, as they left the quayside, heading towards the open sea. From the look on his colleagues faces, Midshipman Pollard was feeling far more exhilarated than the others, and the seaman in charge of delivering them to their post, quickly put John's mind at rest.

"Aye sir, she's one of the finest the navy's got," he explained, "An 80-gun tiered ship of the line, which next to the Victory, in my opinion, cannot be surpassed. But there yee are gentlemen, see for yourself."

All three young officers followed the helmsman's eyeline and could not help but be impressed by the magnificent sight in the distance, on what was to be their home for the foreseeable future. She sat low in the water, gleaming with pride. Her gun covers were up, but the cannons hadn't been run out. As they drew closer, John could see crewmen working on the riggings and sails, like a multitude of flies caught in a spider's web. He sensed that the ship was a hive of activity, being prepared to go to sea. To go to war.

As they approached the Culloden's portside, young Pollard commented to the other two junior officers, with a look of excitement in his eyes, "She looks absolutely splendid."

"Aye, she does at that," the helmsman replied, waving up at the quarter deck for the appropriate lines to be cast down, "She's got twenty-eight 32-pounder guns on her gundeck; another twenty-eight 18-pounders on her upper gundeck, and fourteen 9-pounders on her quarterdeck. There's another four of them on her forecastle. Aye, she's a fighting ship alright, sir, and God help the French when she meets up with them."

'And God help us," John thought to himself, preparing to scale up the side of the warship.

To be addressed as 'sir' was going to be something the lad from Plymouth would have to get used to. He still had many questions to ask, including the reason why, after spending only a year working as a cabin boy on a sloop, one of the navy's smallest warships, he was now a midshipman on one of their largest and most threatening ships of the line. The answer, unknown to him, was that Britain was facing her most-deadliest enemy, and the Admiralty had found it necessary to provide its ships with as many trained seamen, pressed men, and officers as possible, including individuals they only assumed were of officer material. That included former cabin boys of good report.

As he took hold of the rope and began to climb up the side of the awesome looking vessel, he reminded himself to initially pay attention to everything he was told and only speak when requested. He was about to return to that other world where the language was different to what he'd been used to over the past couple of years, and the men he would be responsible for, would be well versed in every devious ploy they could think of to obtain any advantage, especially over a junior officer, so young in service.

The Culloden had a crew of over five hundred men, not including the ship's compliment of officers. The total number of midshipmen on board was six, including John himself and the two newly recruited young men who boarded at Portsmouth. Three other, more experienced officers, had already been recorded in the ship's personnel log.

Once on board, the three most recent additions to the officers list were shown to their berths, and John Pollard was expecting to find better conditions than those he had endured as a cabin boy on the Havik. He was soon to be disappointed. The orlop, which was the lowest deck above the hold, in a vaporous, clammy space forward of the mizzen mast, accommodated midshipmen, masters' mates, surgeons' mates and other petty officers. It was in this dark and smelly part of the ship, where Midshipman Pollard was instructed to hang a hammock, next to the other midshipmen. Limited space was allocated for eating, sleeping and leisure time, well below the water line, the only light coming from tallow tips, the stench of which mingled with the odours of bilge water, rotting timber and seeping foodstuffs coming from stored casks.

The three midshipmen already in residence were sitting around a small table with a lit tallow propped up in the centre. They were just dark figures, lit up only by vague flickering reflections coming from the candle. Their silence added to their resemblance to three ghostly apparitions. Then the quietness of the moment was disturbed by a loud enthusiastic voice.

"My God, I know this gentleman." It came from out of the shadows surrounding the table, "It's the cabin boy off the Havik."

Pollard looked closely at the pale face sitting at the far end of the crudely built wooden table, and instantly recognised Midshipman Smiley, with whom he had depended on so much when serving under Captain Bartholomew.

"John Pollard," the newcomer announced, thrilled to see the man he had regarded as a friend.

"Of course, Pollard," Smiley answered, "Welcome aboard the Culloden, Pollard. Meet your fellow midshipmen."

The more experienced young officer stood and introduced his two colleagues, Henry Batson and Royston Crane, who each nodded at the mention of their names.

"And who, pray tell me, have we here?"

The two recruits who had accompanied the former cabin boy, introduced themselves as being, Thomas Cotton and Timothy Lumb, both looking like frightened spaniels just about to face the unknown.

"Then welcome aboard to you two also. It now appears gentlemen, we have a full pack in the junior officers' berth, and I can only hope that you newcomers are as stout and resilient as Batson and Crane, when we go about destroying the French navy."

Smiley's boisterous confidence had not gone astray, and Pollard's enthusiasm was reignited by the knowledge that such a man would once again, be at his side, only this time, as his equal.

Chapter Five

Three days out from Portsmouth, the crew of HMS Culloden learned they were to become part of Admiral John Jervis's Mediterranean Fleet, with orders to maintain a blockade on the port of Brest, in which a number of French warships had sought refuge. It was a strategy agreed by the Lords of the Admiralty to force the enemy's warships to remain in harbour, by detailing British ships to keep them hemmed in and Brest was France's major sea port. Also, it was feared that Spain would eventually side with Napoleon, which would stretch the Mediterranean Fleet to blockading Cadiz, deploying the same tactics against the Spanish navy. Nevertheless, that situation was yet to arise.

Captain Christopher Cole had been allocated HMS Culloden and as his ship entered the choppy waters of the Bay of Biscay with set courses and top gallants, he sent for his youngest officer for the customary introduction and advice. The meeting was similar to that shared with Captain Bartholomew on the Havik, and Midshipman Pollard was shown into his new captain's quarters by the marine posted outside the cabin door.

Cole was younger than Bartholomew and appeared to be more affable. He began by expressing his regret at the final demise of John Pollard's last berth, before examining the midshipman's personal enlistment papers.

"I see that you served as a cabin boy on the Havik?" he confirmed.

"Yes sir," Pollard answered, remaining stood in front of the captain's desk.

"You must therefore have been wondering how fate has led you to being promoted to your current rank?"

"I am most appreciative, but I had been wondering sir..."

"Well then, you were written up most favourably by both lieutenants on your last ship, as hard working, trustworthy and intelligent. Does that surprise you, young sir?"

"Yes sir, very much so."

"The first thing I advise you to always remember is that, as a King's officer, you no longer have shipmates as such. Your duty is to me and your fellow officers, is that clear?"

"Aye, aye sir."

"Although I personally abhor stripping a man to his waist, and marking the flesh on his back with the lash, discipline is an absolute necessity in the navy. Having said that, whenever you recommend a crew member for punishment, always consider two matters of importance. Firstly, is the offence committed worthy of flogging and secondly, is it of such severity the punishment should be inflicted in the presence of the ship's company, as a deterrent to others. Is that clear?"

"Yes sir."

"Then all I have to offer you Midshipman Pollard, is to continue to work hard, be loyal at all times to your captain, and start studying for your examination to lieutenant, sooner rather than later."

"Yes sir, thankyou sir."

"I am confident you will become a valued member of my crew; dismissed."

"Thank you, sir."

The young man left the captain's cabin, with the impression that Captain Cole was a respected disciplinarian but fair in his judgement. He certainly gave the impression he would not flinch when under pressure, or in the midst of a battle.

Following that formal introductory meeting, the young officer made his way towards the stern, where he had been instructed to report to the second lieutenant, William Briggs. It was then, as he was negotiating the quarter deck, he was unexpectedly confronted by a friendly face. Jack McCreadie was hauling in a line, when the midshipman called his name.

"Blimey, if it's not young Jonno the cabin boy," McCreadie cried out, before realising he was speaking out of turn, "I beg pardon sir, you're an officer now."

"I thought you told me you were set on avoiding the press gang, Jack?" Pollard said, with surprise still written across his young face, and speaking out of earshot of other crew members.

"I did my best, sir," McCreadie answered quietly, putting an emphasis on the last word, "But they eventually got hold of me inside a tavern where I was holed up."

Both men chuckled, confirming their friendship had never faltered, despite the difference there now existed in ranks.

"But look at you," the older man whispered, "How come you're a midshipman on the Culloden?"

"Your guess is as good as mine, Jack."

"Well, I'm the one to keep a secret, so it goes without saying if..."

"I know that Jack, and I appreciate you being here. It's just that..."

"I know sir. We best keep our distance, but as I said, I'm always here should you want to talk in confidence like."

Pollard nodded his approval, and stepped away to report to Lieutenant Briggs for further orders. He wasn't sure whether his past association with McCreadie would prove to be a blessing or hindrance. But he placed a great deal of trust in the man who had supported him during those difficult early days at sea on the Havik. He then decided it would be a blessing.

His first assignment of men was the cleaning detail, and the young midshipman supervised the scrubbing and scraping of all top decks until they were gleaming white. During practice drills, following the order to 'clear for action' his detail would hastily cover all decks with sand, which would remain throughout any action with enemy ships. Nevertheless, being only a drill, at the conclusion the sand had to be swept up and replaced back in the buckets, before the decks would once again have to be scrubbed spotlessly clean. It was a laborious routine, but absolutely essential.

Every Royal Navy ship experienced the same set of circumstances, having recently put together a new crew. It would quickly become clear which amongst the men had been pressed into service, and those who were experienced seamen, the former initially having to be led to their various tasks and instructed as to their duties. The gun crews were mostly made up of seasoned sailors under the supervision of the second and third lieutenants, who were constantly engaged in training and rehearsing against a time piece. Frequently, ropes with knots tied on the end were brought into play, striking men's backs to encourage more speed and efficiency. By the time the ship reached the Bay of Biscay, the First Lieutenant, Richard Johnson, was in a position to report to the captain that the crew had attained levels of satisfaction.

When HMS Culloden finally joined the other ships of the line, blockading Brest, a mist was beginning to develop, but visibility was still sufficient to send ship to ship signals. Captain Cole was directed to the position to be taken in the fleet by the flagship of Admiral Jervis. After that last order had been finalised, another signal was received, requesting the Captain to join the Admiral. Midshipman Pollard watched from the quarter deck as Cole's brig was called for.

During the captain's absence, the mist thickened quickly into a dense fog, as the dusk was turning into night. The below watch had been dismissed, leaving the Dog Watch up top, and it was the First Lieutenant who sent for both Midshipmen Pollard and Smiley. Both young men reported to the officer on the poop deck at the stern, and were instructed to take telescopes up the aft mizzen mast and keep a constant watch on the passage in and out of Brest, as best they could in the surrounding fog.

At first, the young officers' instructions appeared to be impossible to carry out, considering visibility was almost down to zero when they left the deck. However, once they had made the platform high up the mizzen mast, visibility became patchier, as if the fog was clinging to the surface of the sea. It was still black all around them, but at least they could make out a few vague lights coming from other ships of the fleet.

Lieutenant Johnson had been correct to suspect the weather conditions would be ideal for any French ship to attempt exiting the harbour unseen, and he required young eyes to watch for such an effort. The lieutenant was also of the opinion, that out of all the midshipmen on board, Smiley and Pollard were the two most trustworthy.

Both look outs watched as the captain's brig returned to the sound of pipes, as the man in charge regained the quarter-deck, before disappearing down into his cabin, followed by his First Lieutenant.

"What do you think went on between the skipper and admiral?" Pollard asked Arthur Smiley, both men still scrutinising Brest harbour.

"Dinner, glasses of wine and then orders as to what the ship is to be doing in the next few days," the more experienced of the two guessed.

"What I would have given to have been a fly on the wall at that meeting."

"Why be so concerned my friend? Whatever orders were relayed, we shall soon find out whether we are to remain here or be sent to another trouble area, far away."

They both quietly giggled, never taking their telescopes away from their eyes. Six bells rang out from the deck below, and nothing more was said, as they concentrated on fulfilling their task. Although the fog remained fairly dense below their position, they were able to acquire some restricted visibility from where they crouched. It wasn't long before the cold night air began to make its presence felt, with both young officers feeling their cloaks being penetrated sufficiently to make them both wish now they were below decks in their hammocks.

It was Smiley who first brought his fellow officer's attention to some unusual movement he had seen near to the mouth of the harbour.

"What do you think Pollard? Is it my eyes deceiving me or what?"

Pollard concentrated his glass on the vague outline of the coastline, and initially could see only the blackness of the night. But then glanced one single dim light, which could easily have been mistaken for a breaker. He rubbed his eyes, before peering across the surface of the sea, again. He could barely make out a ship's mast, moving slowly and silently out of the harbour, before turning to southward.

"It's a Frenchie," he gasped.

"Look out to the deck," Smiley yelled down to the officer below.

"What have you Mr. Smiley?" the second lieutenant, William Briggs, calmly enquired.

"A Frenchie sir, leaving Brest, with what looks like three masts and all sails set sir."

"Give me a definite bearing Mr. Smiley. Call for the captain on deck if you please Mr. Grey, and all hands, all hands."

Suddenly, the ship burst into action with men swarming on to the decks and taking up various positions around the masts. Whilst Midshipman Smiley kept his telescope fixed on the moving enemy ship, John Pollard saw Lieutenant Briggs climb the rigging of the main mast, before confirming it was a frigate displaying the French flag.

"Clear for action," Lieutenant Johnson ordered, after the captain had joined him on the poop deck.

"Signals; a red flare if you please," the captain instructed.

As the night sky lit up to warn the rest of the fleet that an attempt was being made by the French to leave Brest, men could be seen on the rigging, unfurling the sails on all three masts. Each of the gun decks were covered in sand, and both gunpowder and buckets of water were hurriedly placed at the side of each cannon.

"Cleared for action sir," the First Lieutenant could be heard informing the captain.

It was time for the two midshipmen to return to the quarter deck, and Smiley immediately reported to the captain that the enemy vessel was heading in a southerly direction, apparently on a set course.

"Set course and gallants Mr. Johnson, if you please," the captain instructed.

The sails quickly filled and the speed at which the 170 foot in length Culloden, which weighed 1693 tons. got underway surprised Pollard, who was excited by the prospect of his first involvement with the enemy.

The 36-gun British frigate HMS Antropos joined the Culloden in chasing the French frigate away from Brest, out towards the Atlantic. The wind didn't favour the pursuers, but for six hours they managed to stay in touch with their prey. As dawn was approaching beneath a featureless grey sky, and assisted by the Atlantic winds, the smaller and quicker Antropos finally caught up with their quarry.

John Pollard watched from the bow, as the Antropos engaged the frigate in the distance, waiting for the Culloden to make ground. The sound of rolling thunder could be heard and the midshipman could see the orange flashes, as both ships exchanged cannon fire. It appeared the British vessel was getting the worst of the initial confrontation, but at least she had served her purpose by slowing down the Frenchie.

As Culloden approached the ongoing skirmish, from a position on the enemy's starboard side, and with the Antropos engaging on her port side, the French frigate turned her guns on the 80-gun threat, firing a broadside, which sent Pollard diving to the floor of the deck. One strike hit one of the forward cannons on Culloden, causing it to explode and killing instantly each of its five-man crew, wounding others.

The young midshipman found himself screaming at crew members to take the injured below deck to the surgeon. And yet, the order to fire wasn't yet given by the Culloden's captain. She drew closer, turning to position herself for a retaliatory broadside, and when she was in a favourable position, the order finally came to open fire. Lieutenant Johnson was by then on the top gun decks supervising the cannon, with the other lieutenants positioned on the lower tiers.

The French frigate was no match for Culloden's fire power, as the British warship spewed out death and destruction, enveloping both ships in clouds of black smoke. The youngest of the midshipmen could see bodies of Frenchmen flying through the air, with fragments of wood confirming the severity of the damage being caused. The enemy's fore mast and rigging came crashing down on to her decks, and her main mast leant back at an odd angle, adding to her distress. Following another broadside, her resistance began to weaken.

After each attack, the guns were quickly brought back in and swamped with water to cool the barrels before the reloading process began again. Only the top sails were now unfurled, allowing Culloden to match the slowness of the enemy frigate. The second broadside delivered was sufficient to totally disable the Frenchie's manoeuvrability.

"Mr. Briggs," Captain Cole called out above the general din, "Select your boarding party; pistols and cutlasses if you please."

"Aye, aye sir, pistols and cutlasses."

A total of one hundred of the crew members were ordered to take their weapons from the wooden chests brought up from below deck, and together with the same number of marines, the boarding party was ready within a few minutes. Both Pollard and Smiley were included.

As Culloden moved in closer to its crippled target, she was met with only musket fire, and as soon as both vessels made physical contact, Lieutenant Briggs led the charge by leaping across to the frigate, followed by the armed men. John Pollard also leapt across the small gap, grasping a sword in one hand, and a loaded pistol in the other.

When the youngest member of the crew landed on the crowded, noisy deck of the Frenchie, he was immediately attacked by two dark blurry figures, both wearing blue tops with white straps across their chests, obviously the French's equivalent to the red coated marines. Looking both fearful and angry, he fired a ball into the face of one of his assailant's, and decapitated the other with his cutlass. For minutes rather than hours, Pollard fought like a mad man, slashing and thrusting; slashing and thrusting, bringing down a fair number of the enemy defenders, until finally he raised his sword up in the air in readiness to strike yet again. Only, it was the grime covered face of a British marine staring back at him.

"Steady sir," the man called out, bringing an immediate end to Pollard's obsession with killing or be killed.

A bloodstained Lieutenant Briggs stood at the midshipman's side, ordering his men to cease fighting. The remaining crew of Frenchmen were huddled together around the lob sided main mast protruding from the quarter deck, having been disarmed. They numbered no more than thirty, with the same number of red coats surrounding them, all pointing muskets directly at the captured enemy. It was over. Midshipman Pollard had successfully fought in his first hand-to-hand confrontation, and only then, still feeling the exhilaration of combat, took time to survey the surrounding scene. It was a gathering of dead and wounded, strewn across the decks and accompanied by groans and cries. Some bloodied bodies were hanging from the enemy ship's rigging, and others straddled across unworkable cannons; the majority being enemy seamen. Many of the dead had sustained horrific injuries and the young man was seeing for the first time, the reality of war.

He called out for Midshipman Smiley, but received no response. Then through the smoke and haze, he sighted his friend lying on his back on the deck, unconscious. Arthur Smiley appeared to be dead, and Pollard rushed across to him, cradling his friend in his arms and calling out his name. There was still no response, but the young man was breathing. After summoning help from other members of the boarding party, including an exhausted looking Jack McCreadie, the severely wounded midshipman was carried back across to the Culloden with other injured seamen, and quickly transferred to the care of the ship's surgeon. There were tears in Pollard's eyes and he unashamedly begged the ship's surgeon to save his friend. But it was doubtful Smiley would survive the day.

Chapter Six

The damage sustained to HMS Culloden was minimal following the skirmish with the French frigate, L'Invincible', except for the loss of one cannon and the surrounding rail. She took some additional damage to her stern, but nothing the ship's carpenter couldn't put right. The enemy ship was in a far more serious condition. She had lost two of her masts. The frigate, L'Invincible, was also without helm control, and had to be towed into Portsmouth with the remains of a heavily guarded crew kept on board. Although capable of being sea worthy, the Atropos had sustained heavy casualties and damage to her main mast. It was decided, following the burials at sea, she would also accompany Culloden into dock for repairs. What prize money would be obtained from the sale of L'Invincible was to be shared amongst the two British crews, but that was the last thing on Midshipman Pollard's mind.

It was a forlorn and extremely worried young officer who visited Arthur Smiley, being cared for by the ship's surgeon, Albert Cross, in an allocated space tween decks. At least his friend was still alive, and he wasn't surprised to find both the surgeon and ship's captain in attendance. Reluctant to interrupt what appeared to be an ongoing conversation between the two officers and injured man, he stopped just short of where his fellow midshipman was lying. When Captain Cole sighted Pollard, he immediately beckoned him to advance to his friend's bedside.

Smiley lay there on his back, with an ashen face and most of the upper part of his body covered in bandaging. Pollard could just about hear him whisper to the captain, enquiring whether they had secured a victory.

"Yes, victory is ours," the most senior officer confirmed, "But don't concern yourself with that at present, Mr. Smiley."

"I did my duty sir," the injured man suggested, in a quiet croaking voice.

"Yes, that you did Mr. Smiley, and now you must allow the surgeon to do his."

"Will I be in much pain doctor?" Smiley asked, showing he was already in a great deal of pain from the distortion in his facial features. The young man was extremely fearful, which was not surprising in the dire circumstances.

"I won't lie to you Mr. Smiley, you will be, but I shall administer something to ease that for you," the surgeon explained, "Including a large amount of rum."

"I don't drink though sir."

"Then might I suggest it's time you began."

The captain turned to leave, offering to bring Mr. Smiley a number of books to read, which he believed the young man would find interesting during the time he would spend recovering from the operation about to be performed.

The surgeon also left, but as he followed the captain spoke quietly to Pollard, advising him not to remain too long, as there was an urgent need to perform surgery sooner rather than later.

"They are taking my arm, below the elbow" the wounded midshipman told his visitor, who had nothing but sympathy for his friend, and noticed a small tear trickling down one side of his face.

"Then the surgeon must think it's necessary to do so, Arthur."

"Yes."

"None of us thought you would make it to here. Is there anything I can get you?"

"No, except of course, a new replacement arm."

Pollard nodded, smiling down at his young friend.

"Will you do me the honour Pollard, of remaining with me when the doctor performs his duty?"

"Of course, as long as the surgeon is agreeable."

Smiley nodded and appeared to relax more at that point, closing his eyes and resting, obviously not looking forward to the drama that was about to unfold. The young man had been heavily dosed with laudanum, and there would be a lot more of the opium-based drug administered before the operation commenced. But there could be no delay, as it was fairly common for gangrene to set in when a severe wound had been inflicted. Arthur Smiley's lower arm had been smashed to pieces, leaving him with multiple wounds and increasing the chances of infection already present. There was no alternative but to remove the affected limb. Even after that course of action had been undertaken, it would be touch and go whether the young patient would survive the ordeal.

With both the surgeon and his mate in attendance around the bedside, there was little room for the younger midshipman to remain, but, as he had promised his wounded friend, he was determined to do so, standing to one side as an observer. After placing a number of instruments on a small table beside the makeshift bed, Albert Cross instructed his assistant to administer more laudanum to the patient. He then waited a few seconds for the drug to take effect, before nodding at the other medical man, who stepped around the table, placing both hands on each side of Smiley's head.

"How are you feeling now young man?" the doctor enquired.

"I've known better sir," Smiley grimaced, in a slurred voice, having also just tasted his first tumbler full of rum.

"Yes, well I shall act with all speed." Surgeon Cross then nodded towards John Pollard, signalling for him to assist by holding the patient down, once the surgery commenced.

As soon as the sharpness of the scalpel was felt just below the left elbow, Arthur Smiley screamed out in agony. John Pollard grasped the other arm and held it down, also leaning across the patient's torso to avoid as little movement as possible. Blood was splattered everywhere, even though a tourniquet had been secured above the elbow of the injured arm.

The screams reverberated around the ship and much of the ongoing work on the top decks and rigging stopped momentarily. It was a rare moment when the men were not encouraged to continue with their work. Even the officers appeared to be shaken by the young patient's cries for mercy.

"Oh God Almighty," the injured young man called out, with the surgeon's assistant using all his strength to avoid the patient from moving his head.

Smiley was unable to see the teeth of the saw in the surgeon's hand, and Pollard winced as the sound of the bones below Smiley's elbow were attended to. Within a minute of the first cut, the arm was removed and thrown into a nearby bucket, before the surgeon got to work, covering the open wound with some kind of cleansing powder. The needle and thread followed, and by that time, thankfully, the patient was unconscious.

After wrapping the open wound with more padding and bandages, the surgeon finally looked up and thanked both men for their assistance.

"He mustn't be moved for at least a week, to give time for the amputation to heal. The only problem our friend here is likely to face is if infection sets in." Turning to his assistant, he continued, handing over a large bottle containing a white liquid substance, "He is to be given a large gulp of this, four times a day Jacob, until I say otherwise."

The assistant nodded his understanding, and then John Pollard left to vomit in a wooden bucket. He had also felt Smiley's pain and was exhausted after his ordeal.

The next few days following the surgery would be the most important in Arthur Smiley's fight to survive, and during that time the dressings were changed frequently and the laudanum administered sparingly.

By the time Culloden and Atropos reached Portsmouth, with the French frigate in tow, the injured midshipman had got over the worst, and actually managed to climb through a hatchway and gain the quarter deck with some help from Pollard. Smiley felt good to breathe in the fresh sea air once again, and such a diversion was repeated on a daily basis, even when the ship was in dry dock for repairs to be completed. The one-armed midshipman was the only member of the ship allowed to disembark to visit a hospital on shore for regular check-ups, and on one occasion, as a favour requested by his friend, visited Thomas and Rose Pollard in Plymouth. In a strange way, he was proud of the one empty sleeve of his uniform jacket, confirming he had actually been in battle.

He stayed for almost an hour with the Pollards, drinking tea and informing them that all was well with young John. They were both appreciative of the young officer's visit, and Smiley left them in good heart.

Admiral Jervis had been informed of the position of both British ships by way of dispatches taken out to the flagship every week, and Culloden remained at Portsmouth for the following three weeks. During that period and before the repaired ship of the line could return to the fleet, Spain declared war on Britain. With an alliance between France and Spain, Napoleon's occupation of most of Europe, placed into perspective the enormity of the threat the French Emperor had become to England, and of course, to the peace of the world. It quickly came to the notice of the Lords of the Admiralty that plans for invasion were being made across the channel. And yet, Britain's enemy still had the daunting task of defeating her navy, before any French soldier could place one foot on English soil.

Culloden was ordered to re-join Jervis's fleet in the Mediterranean, and during the voyage southwards towards Gibraltar, yet another distressing incident was experienced by the young midshipman from Plymouth.

Captain Cole had been replaced by Sir Thomas Troubridge as captain of HMS Culloden. The new senior officer had a vast experience in warfare at sea, having fought at the Battle of the Hyères Islands, and having led the line at the Battle of Cape St Vincent. Captain Troubridge had also served with Horatio Nelson in the East Indies, and on one occasion had been captured by the French, although he was released shortly after his incarceration, and returned to England.

"Something is brewing, trust me," Midshipman Smiley remarked, as he stood on the quarter deck with John Pollard, both watching the distant lights of Portsmouth slowly fading in the darkness of the night.

"What makes you think that?" his friend enquired, again feeling melancholic, having been so close to his father and sister, but unable to leave the ship and pay his personal respects. At least Smiley had served to represent him at the small terraced house in Plymouth for which Pollard was extremely thankful, being given assurance that his small family were well and in good heart.

"There's always something major brewing when we have a change of captain, and I think it's something to do with Sir Thomas being a close friend of Admiral Nelson. The other thing is, why are we leaving the channel fleet to return to Admiral Jervis in the Mediterranean?"

"How do you know we are?"

"I overheard the First Lieutenant telling the boatswain on the poop deck earlier. Lieutenant Johnson reckons there are plans to attack a major Spanish port in an effort to disable their navy."

"Christ Arthur, how will you manage with one arm when we go into action?"

"As long as I can hold a cutlass in my hand, I shall do my duty, have no fear of that. By the way, have you heard about Batson being attacked by one of the crew?" Henry Batson was another midshipman who was virtually as experienced as Smiley, except the individual had gained a reputation for being heavy-handed towards the men in his charge.

"No, but I'm not surprised the way the man dishes out punishment more gleefully than the Boatswain. What happened?"

"I feel sorry for the poor blighter. Apparently, Batson was beating on a cabin boy, when one of the men told him to stop. When he turned to strike the same man with his cane, he was punched in the face."

"My God, that calls for instant death." Pollard was referring to the mandatory sentence imposed on a crew member for striking an officer. Such an act would leave a captain with no other option but to hang the offender from the yardarm, in full view of the remainder of the crew.

"Exactly, the seaman was immediately dragged before a court martial in Portsmouth and sentenced to be hanged without delay, the time being at the discretion of the captain. The execution is to take place in the morning at six bells; we're all to be present. I'm surprised you haven't been told, Pollard."

Culloden had set her royals as a slight breeze in the channel greeted the following morning. Dawn was on the horizon, diluting the darkness of the previous night to a murky grey. Every member of the ship's company was crowded on to all decks, and the captain stood in front of his officers on the quarter deck. A drum roll began as the condemned prisoner was brought up from the hold by two grim looking red-coated marines. Both hands and feet were secured by chains, and he was wearing his navy issue white shirt with white trousers.

No one, including the captain ever looked forward to seeing a man dangle in mid-air with a rope around his neck, and all heads were bowed, as the condemned man was met by the First Lieutenant, Richard Johnson.

John Pollard gasped when he stared at the face of the man about to be lawfully executed. The prisoner was none other than his loyal and trusted friend, Jack McCreadie. The young midshipman wanted to cry out; to stop the inevitable, and his mouth opened to call out his dissent.

"No John," the one-armed Arthur Smiley whispered to him, standing at his side, "Don't be a fool, there is nothing you can do."

Pollard's mouth closed, and his eyes began to well up.

"Retain your dignity," his friend added, in such a quiet way, no other crew member or officer could overhear the warning.

Immediately, the distressed midshipman inhaled a deep breath, as the First Lieutenant requested the captain for permission to carry out the sentence imposed by the court martial back in Portsmouth.

"Carry on, Mr. Johnson, if you please," Captain Troubridge solemnly ordered from where he stood.

The officer turned to the prisoner and declared in a loud voice, "Seaman McCreadie, you have been found guilty by a lawfully arranged naval court of striking one of His Majesty's Royal Naval officers, for which the penalty is death, and for which you have been duly sentenced. Have you anything you wish to say before sentence is carried out?"

McCreadie shook his bowed head, before the chains around both ankles were replaced by rope, maintaining his restricted movement.

The First Lieutenant nodded, and yet another drum roll reverberated around the vessel.

The prisoner was escorted by the same two marines up to the yard-arm and a noose was placed around his neck, the line of which ran through a tackle hanging down from a large pole positioned across the mast. Still, the condemned man remained silent, and the lieutenant in charge nodded towards six of McCreadie's shipmates grasping the line. Each of them looked regretful, as they began to haul away on the rope, dragging James McCreadie upwards, until both of his feet left the deck. Kicking and choking, the body of the wretched seaman hung just below the yard-arm, where it was left secured. All in attendance were forced to watch as the convicted man's feet continued to twitch, his life slowly ebbing away, and bringing it to a gruesome end.

Never before in his young life had John Pollard witnessed such a barbaric and tortuous act under the label of naval discipline. Even after the company had been dismissed following the lawful execution, he remained glued to the same spot, staring across at the hanging corpse of his friend and companion. Smiley remained at his side, not speaking a word and understanding the pain his fellow officer must have been feeling. This was retribution at its harshest; its most cruel; its most wicked, and although considered by many critics as unnecessary, that was not the view of the Lords of the Admiralty, back in London.

Throughout the remainder of that day, as the ship continued to head southwards, Midshipman Pollard had to forcibly avert his eyes away from Jack McCreadie's hanging body, each time he went on deck to continue with his own duties. It wasn't until the following evening that the captain ordered the condemned man's body to be cut down and buried at sea, much to Pollard's relief. The young man from Plymouth would never forget the friend who had been his nursemaid, when serving on Havik, and watched over him during the time they had been together on HMS Culloden. He despised his fellow midshipman who had been responsible for ending McCreadie's life, but had learned sufficiently by then to keep his own counsel. But for John Pollard, life in His Majesty's service would never be the same again.

By the time the ship reached the Mediterranean Fleet, rumours regarding the actions they were about to become engaged in, had already spread around the vessel like wild fire. According to some, they were going to be part of a squadron of fighting ships tasked with attacking some of the French ships of war. Other misleading tales alleged skirmishes were to take place on land, in attempts to nullify various shore batteries belonging to the French and Spanish.

In fact, having taken its position amongst the fleet, HMS Culloden did very little, except remain at anchor, although it was noticeable how much time Captain Troubridge spent away from the ship, responding to requests for his attendance on Admiral Jervis's flag ship, HMS London.

During the second week spent beneath the warm Mediterranean sun, finally, the ship was cleared for action.

Having already tasted the tragedy of battle, Midshipman Pollard wasn't as enthusiastic on this occasion about confronting other enemy ships, and for the first time since joining the navy, wished he was elsewhere.

Chapter Seven

Admiral Jervis had received intelligence that the island of Tenerife was frequently the recipient of convoys from America, transporting Spanish treasure. Fishermen working in and around the Canary Islands also confirmed what had been regarded as a closely kept secret. As a result, he dispatched two reconnoitring frigates in search of the reported convoys. It was a surprise to the Admiral when his ships successfully captured two French and Spanish vessels in a night-time raid, near to the Tenerife coastline. No treasure was recovered, but encouraged by that recent success, the Admiral decided to seize Santa Cruz, Tenerife's major port located in the northeast quadrant of the island.

Jervis planned to achieve his ambition by means of an amphibious attack, using both seamen and marines, and if successful, the operation would be looked upon with great pleasure and satisfaction by the Lords of the Admiralty. Even more so, if gold and other treasure was eventually seized to help pay for Britain's participation in the war.

It was during the planning stage of the intended attack on the Spanish port, that an incident took place on the Culloden that considerably affected the crews' morale, at a time when it should have been at its highest level, with the ship having been cleared for action. The hanging of James McCreadie from the yardarm, had obviously not deterred Midshipman Henry Batson from continuing to apply his birching cane sparingly. In fact, the young officer had replaced his 'rattan' − a single strip of cane, with three similar strips. He had in fact, adapted his instrument of torture to inflict even greater pain on his victims, making no secret of his intentions. The junior officer did not have to wait too long, before having the opportunity to test his new device.

As one of the powder boys was bringing a barrel filled with cartridges up from below, he slipped on the deck. Fortunately, nothing was spilt and the young lad was careful to place his burden next to one of the cannons being attended by a gun crew.

Matthew Brown, one of the gunners on the quarter deck, advised the powder boy not to rush when responding to a clear for action order.

"Aye lad, it's far better to take a few more seconds to get there in one piece than not at all. One bad slip, and the whole bleedin' ship could go up."

"Yes sir, sorry sir," the lad answered, having his hair tousled by Brown's fatherly hand, who told him to be on his way and continue bringing up more supplies for some of the other guns.

As the boy turned to go back down the hatch, he was confronted by Midshipman Batson, standing on the deck with both legs apart and hands behind his back, grasping his newly adapted three-pronged rattan. The youngster looked up in horror, realising what his immediate fate was to be, before being hurriedly dragged by his collar across the deck to the base of some of the rigging.

"Your clumsiness has put the whole ship in danger," the midshipman screamed at the lad, "Strip to the waist."

The unfortunate, tearful miscreant did as he was ordered, and both of his small hands were strapped to the rigging. He cried out as each dried reed of the cane cut into his tender and fragile young white back. Five, six, seven lashes were sufficient to scar the youngster's exposed spine, and still the birching continued; nine, ten, eleven, the punishment being applied with all the gusto Midshipman Baston could muster. The boy's back was by then a mass of bloody stripes.

"I think the boys had enough, sir." It was Matthew Brown coming to the victim's aid, "Shall I take him down below now sir, to see the surgeon?"

Midshipman Batson turned to face the crew member who had displayed sufficient courage to interrupt the punishment. His eyes were those of a madman, staring directly into the gunner's.

"What did you say?" the officer said, in a threatening voice.

"Beg pardon sir, but he's only a youngster and he's learned his lesson."

"Sergeant," Batson yelled to one of the marines nearby, "Two men if you please, to escort this impudent and worthless soul to the hold. I shall be present shortly."

Gunner Brown was physically taken below by two of the red coated marines, watched by the whole on-duty crew, including both Pollard and Smiley, who were near to the taffrail at the stern of the ship.

"He does seem to enjoy inflicting pain on the hands," Midshipman Pollard remarked quietly.

"Yes, he does and one of these days our Mr. Batson is going to get what he deserves," Smiley commented.

The powder boy received another three lashes, before Batson ordered him to be cut down, impatient to follow the marines who had taken Matthew Brown down into the hold. Following his severe punishment, the youngster wasn't fit for duty and was carried by a shipmate down to his bunk to recover. A few minutes after the deck had been cleared, the two midshipmen watching from the poop deck, were surprised by another unusual sight.

Matthew Brown appeared back on deck and slowly made his way back to the remainder of his gun crew. Each of them looked stunned at what stood before them. A large bolt and nut had been placed into the gunner's mouth and was held secure by a piece of rag tied around the back of his head. The man's hands were tethered around his back, and he sat on the deck next to his cannon. He was helpless, unable to do anything with both wrists bound together.

"My God, what on earth as that bloody maniac done now?" Arthur Smiley enquired.

"He's been gagged, Arthur," Pollard said, describing the obvious.

"And what if we went into action this very minute, how would he be able to perform his duty?"

"If that was to be the case, I would personally remove that gag," Pollard swore.

An hour passed by with the Culloden remaining cleared for action, and during which time, Matthew Brown stayed crouched at the side of his gun, barely breathing. His face was blue and he was obviously in distress, so much so, Midshipman Pollard reported the matter to the Second Lieutenant, William Briggs, requesting that Brown's breathing obstruction should be removed immediately.

"I'm afraid the man spoke out of turn to an officer when inflicting punishment Mr. Pollard," Briggs explained, "To interfere with any subsequent punishment would be folly sir, and most certainly in breach of navy regulations."

After two hours following the bolt and nut being placed inside Brown's mouth, he rolled over sideways on to the deck, with his gunnery shipmates watching. He was dead, having been asphyxiated. Those who had witnessed the entire incident, unable to assist the wretched gunner, were now shocked by what had taken place. Enormous derision and hatred quickly built up throughout the whole crew, their venom targeting Midshipman Batson, who continued pacing the decks, as if nothing untoward had happened. There would be yet another funeral, resulting from the overzealous and masochistic activities of the man with the rattan.

"I'll see the bastard hang for this," John Pollard swore.

"No, you won't Pollard," Smiley advised, "You heard what Lieutenant Briggs said earlier, and you can rest assured the captain will say the same."

After Captain Troubridge had conducted the appropriate service, prior to Matthew Brown's body being committed to the sea, there was a loud hissing sound, which vibrated around Culloden. It was the crews' way of showing their discontent at the action of the despised Midshipman Batson, who at the time was standing at the side of the captain. Every officer on board Culloden at that moment was aware that such indiscipline could threaten mutiny, and the midshipmen in particular were instructed to quieten down the crew, and subdue the anger being felt as a matter of priority.

A word of caution was shared with the heavy-handed junior officer by Captain Troubridge, but that was all, and the matter was closed. But Gunner Brown would never be forgotten by his shipmates, or some of the officers who had witnessed that appalling spectacle, whilst anchored just outside Gibraltar.

Finally, with Admiral Jervis's approval, plans to seize the port of Santa Cruz, were completed. They consisted of a small squadron participating in the attack under the command of Rear Admiral Horatio Nelson. When the great man himself sailed into Gibraltar in his flagship, HMS Theseus, waves of excitement and anticipation swept through the fleet. Apart from the captains and a few selected senior officers, no one was aware of the details of the operation about to be undertaken.

"One thing is for certain," the First Lieutenant, Richard Johnson, told the two midshipmen, Pollard and Smiley, "With Nelson in charge, where ever we are going, there will most definitely be fireworks."

The squadron ordered by Jervis comprised of the Culloden, HMS Zealous, another 74-gun ship, and three frigates, Seahorse, Emerald and Terpsichore. In addition, the attack force was supported by the cutter, HMS Fox, a mortar boat, the Ray and HMS Leander, a 50-gun ship. Nelson's total armament was 400 guns with approximately 4000 marines and seamen, which he considered was more than sufficient to achieve victory, as the group left Gibraltar.

Although the junior officers and crew of Culloden were still completely unaware of the target or purpose of the newly formed squadron, each of them was certain that, with Nelson leading the way, glory and honour were distinct possibilities.

Unknown to the British, following the earlier capture of the French and Spanish ships off Tenerife, Lieutenant General Antonio Gutierrez, the officer responsible for the defence of the Canary Islands, decided to reinforce his defences, particularly around Santa Cruz. Spanish forts were rebuilt, field works expanded, and shore batteries virtually doubled behind the protection of earth sacks. A force of more than seventeen hundred men were gathered, consisting of soldiers, partisans, militia, artillery, sailors and even local huntsmen in preparation for any intended attack on the port.

Nelson's plan was a basic and simple strategy, one which called for a night-time landing under Captain Troubridge of the Culloden. The three British frigates would stealthily land troops with instructions to take out shore batteries located north-east of Santa Cruz harbour. The firing of a flare would confirm that part of the operation had been successful, when HMS Ray would then attack the city with mortar fire. If all went according to plan, by the time the dawn arrived, Nelson's ships of the line, including HMS Culloden, would enter the harbour and take possession of Spanish merchant ships and valuables. Nelson intended to personally send a note to the Spanish authorities, demanding the surrender of all Spanish cargo, including treasure transported from America, and threatening to destroy the city should his demands not be met. It was without doubt, a daring plan but extremely profitable if concluded successfully.

On the evening before the planned attack, Captain Troubridge boarded the flagship, HMS Theseus to finalise Nelson's plans with the Rear Admiral and other captains. It was decided the attack would take place in two separate phases. The first would involve the landing of a thousand seamen and marines at Valle Seco beach, two miles north of Santa Cruz. That land force would then continue to surround and capture Fort Paso Alto. If the port had not surrendered by that time, the landing party would launch the final attack on the city. Little resistance was expected and Troubridge left Nelson's flagship confident of success.

The following night saw a full moon lighting the way across the waves, which caused Nelson some concern, preferring to launch the attack in complete darkness. Nevertheless, the operation still got underway, with thirty-nine boats each carrying seamen and marines leaving the ships, with midshipmen responsible for smaller groups.

John Pollard found himself in charge of six of the smaller craft, and the one-armed Arthur Smiley led the way across the surface of the water with seven vessels under his charge, grasping his cutlass in one hand. There was an atmosphere of confidence amongst the invasion force, almost edging on the brink of recklessness, each of them expecting little resistance from the shore, as the small flotilla approached the shoreline.

The sky was clear and typical of a summer Canary night, and the first threat to the would-be invaders came when they met strong adverse currents, which frustrated their progress. This was a feature that had not been planned for and a great deal of delay was experienced, as the oarsmen worked hard to overcome the natural phenomenon, without having much success. Pollard became increasingly concerned they would soon lose the element of surprise. The midshipman's fears were realised when the ordinary people of Santa Cruz, noticed the outlines of the enemy vessels in the moonlight, and enthusiastically raised the alarm.

All hell was suddenly unleashed around the invasion force, as the Spanish cannons spewed out death and destruction from their shore batteries. A number of the boats were hit and wrecked. Men took to the water, whilst others were killed by the onslaught. Nelson's vanguard was quickly being pulverised with three of John Pollard's vessels being disintegrated, together with others. The situation was rapidly becoming a losing cause, and it was Midshipman Smiley who shouted across the water to his fellow officer, that they should retreat back to the ships. Remaining under intense fire, the seamen and marines managed to rescue many of the wounded, before leaving the area of bombardment with their tails between their legs. The plan had failed miserably, and well before the execution of the main part of the proposed plan had been afforded any possibility of execution.

Rear Admiral Nelson was infuriated but not defeated. In a second orchestrated attempt to achieve the objective, the British frigates were towed inshore by rowing boats, close to the Bufadero, a natural phenomenon of coastal morphology in cliffs of soluble rocks such as limestone and dolomite. The Paso Alto castle opened fire on the intruders, yet despite the difficult currents and obvious lack of animals to carry artillery to the shore, the British still managed to land over a thousand soldiers on the beach with some equipment.

Unfortunately for the attacking land force, Gutierrez had recruited even more activists, placing them inside the castle to replenish forces transferred from the Santa Cruz fortress. The inevitable outcome was a cannonade and musket onslaught, forcing the troops to be recalled back to the three frigates. Under heavy fire, amazingly the British lost only two men, and once back on board, the Rear Admiral played out yet another card, which was more from desperation. The British frigates began to pound the coastal cliffs with cannon, intending to frighten and silence the enemy, but to no avail. The Spanish defenders were far more resilient than had been anticipated.

Gutierrez was a canny strategist and moved his troops, in particular his artillerymen, to the port batteries, denying the would-be invaders any attempt to overcome the resistance.

Nelson regrouped and called each of his captains to yet another strategy meeting on board the Theseus, declaring that he himself would lead the next move, which would comprise of a direct attack on the San Cristobal castle in Santa Cruz harbour. Again, and unknown to the Rear Admiral, Gutierrez had foreseen Nelson's next move and gathered his best troops back at San Cristobal.

The British still arguably considered the element of surprise was still their most effective ally, and cloth padded oars were used to propel boats containing seven hundred troops into the harbour, during yet another night time raid. As was the case during the first failed attempt to make an amphibious landing, Midshipman Pollard was in charge of some of the boats. Arthur Smiley had the honour of directing the same boat in which Nelson was being transported.

As the small flotilla approached the shoreline, Midshipman Smiley noticed for the first time, a patch over one of the Rear Admiral's eyes. One of the crewmen confirmed their leader had in fact been blinded during earlier fighting in Corsica.

All seemed to be going well, until a Spanish frigate anchored just off the pier, fired an alarm shot as the British attack force drew nearer to the shore. Some of the boats reached the beach, but were targeted by a crossfire of cannon balls and musket bullets fired from the batteries of Paso Alto, San Miguel, San Antonio and San Pedro. The resistance to the invasion attempt was proving to be formidable.

Midshipman Pollard managed to lead a party of marines to Paso Alto and successfully spiked a couple of cannons. But their actions were feeble compared to the resistance of the Spanish, and no matter how much the young midshipman earnestly tried to motivate his men, Spanish mortars and cannons forced their retreat back to the beach. The young officer was dismayed at sight of so many British casualties spread about the shoreline injured or dead.

Midshipman Smiley stood helpless on the beach, when he saw the distressing sight of Horatio Nelson fall on one knee, hit in the arm. The limb was severely damaged and the young officer could see it was bleeding copiously. The midshipman and sailors who had accompanied Nelson were ordered to row furiously back to the Rear Admiral's flagship, with heavy artillery fire raking up the sea around them. It was only good fortune that saw Smiley return his celebrated senior officer to safety.

Amazingly, an angry and dejected Nelson ordered his surgeon to remove the injured limb, which he described as being, 'useless'. The arm was surgically removed and thrown into the sea that same night, bringing an end to Admiral Jervis's orders to take Santa Cruz.

Midshipman Pollard also had similar good fortune, retreating back through a vast cauldron of enemy fire, to reach the safety of the Culloden, but after boarding, he was greeted by an unusual and surprising sight. Midshipman Batson was standing on the quarter deck watching the action from the safety of the ship. Although, he suspected the man had been sufficiently cunning to avoid the recent hostilities, Pollard thought it best not to enquire.

The attack on Santa Cruz had failed, and the British had to accept failure. As a result, the fleet was demoralised, whereby Spanish hearts were uplifted, and their will to continue siding the French against the enemy, became more entrenched than ever before. The defenders suffered only thirty dead and forty injured, while the British lost two hundred and fifty souls, with one hundred and twenty-eight wounded. It had been a bitter miscarriage, and Admiral Jervis, who had expected to see the Union Jack flying over the Spanish port, was furious when he learned of the fiasco. There was never to be another attack on the harbour at Santa Cruz.

Following that first defeat in which HMS Culloden was involved, the one-armed Nelson was forced to return to Britain to recuperate.

In the meantime, Napoleon had made plans to invade Egypt in an introductory attempt to eventually break the link between Britain and India, a country from which goods and supplies were a major source of income to finance their ships at sea.

Vice-Admiral Earl St. Vincent was appointed as commander of the Mediterranean Fleet, and when news was received by the Admiralty in London, that the French were making preparations on the Mediterranean coast, St. Vincent was ordered to dispatch a squadron to investigate. It wouldn't be long before HMS Culloden was once again heading into battle, under the leadership of Rear Admiral Nelson.

Chapter Eight

The effect James McCreadie's death had on John Pollard was immense, and the young man couldn't seem to shake off a dark cloud of depression, which seemed to constantly plague him throughout the days that followed the Santa Cruz debauchery. The distressing experience of seeing Gunner Brown 'gagged' in such a way as to bring about his unfortunate death, also added to the moroseness, which had taken a strong hold on the midshipman. Never before did he imagine such barbaric cruelty existed in Britain's navy, except of course, when in conflict with the enemy.

For the first time in his short naval life, he was questioning his own situation, querying why such dreadful activities should be allowed to take place. Had he been mistaken in rushing to the call from his King, to serve in the most dominant navy in the world. Was the negativity plaguing his mind sourced from reality or perhaps misconstrued. Whatever; the young officer knew he had to somehow eject the predilection of pending disaster from his thoughts quickly, or become immersed in so many doubts he could lose his own sense of certainty and stability.

Pollard gained some encouragement from the manner in which the tragic loss of an arm didn't seem to affect Midshipman Smiley in the least, and he became more and more impressed when seeing his friend bearing his disability so well, and being so committed to his daily duties far more fervently than ever before. The two men became closer to each other, often sharing stories, opinions and snippets of information in confidence, and yet Pollard could not make mention of his own personal nightmares. Allowing for the trauma through which Arthur Smiley had survived, only a sense of immense shame would have accompanied such idiosyncratic disclosure.

Eventually, as the ship slowly returned to some normality following Santa Cruz, Pollard's depression began to lift. It transpired during their conversations that Arthur Smiley had been an orphan before going to sea. Not being a pressed man, and in similar fashion to Midshipman Pollard, he had enlisted, except he had spent twelve months at the naval academy before being promoted to midshipman.

With all the uncertainty and issues teasing the Plymouth man's thought patterns, his preferred watch was that which covered the early evenings, known as the Dog Watch. It seemed that particular period, between day and night, when the sun had gone down and the sea had calmed, the ship enjoyed its quiet and surreal moments. He would often be found on the poop deck deep in thought, unless the captain appeared, resulting in the deck being cleared of officers to allow Captain Troubridge room to pace up and down, whenever the fancy took him. But on this one particular night, following their return to Gibraltar for repairs and supplies, including armament requisitioning, the youngest of the midshipmen was leaning over the rail, alone. He was savouring that rare period of isolation, so difficult to achieve while serving on a crowded ship of the line, when a sudden interruption irked him.

"Dreaming of home?" Smiley enquired in a quiet voice.

If it had been any other midshipman or lower rating disturbing Pollard's serenity, they would have been met with abusive and protesting words. But Mr. Smiley was an exception.

"Not really, although I should be, I suppose," the disturbed young officer answered.

"It doesn't pay to dwell too much on home comforts, not when serving in one of His Majesty's ships of the line my friend."

It was advice which he could very well have done without, but there was a need to remain civil.

"I was thinking more of the country just over on that horizon, Mr. Smiley; Africa."

"What of it?"

"I was wondering what it was like for a country not to be at war. It appears that Africa is the only one, which hasn't declared for or opposed the French and her allies. It's so frustrating to realise England appears to be standing alone against the Corsican tyrant."

Smiley followed his friend's eyeline towards the dark southern horizon, and declared, "It's only a matter of time before I reckon that Devil incarnate will take a fancy to her, and she will have no option but to fight him. Want to hear something interesting?"

"Aye, what have you learned that's brought that smile to your face?" Pollard enquired, now fully out of his reverie.

"Well it's like this see, I overheard Lieutenant Johnson quietly telling the Boatswain that Napoleon has invaded the Island of Malta, where he has resupplied his ships. Again, according to the First Lieutenant, he's currently heading towards Alexandria."

"Where's that Arthur; Greece?"

"No, Egypt."

"Why would he go there?"

"That's the same question the Boatswain asked and Lieutenant Johnson was of the opinion, it's India that Napoleon's after, specifically, British India."

"So, when are we leaving?" Pollard asked, with genuine enthusiasm.

"We're not; not just yet any roads, but the First Lieutenant mentioned there were some preparations being made, and eventually it will be us who will go looking for the Frogs."

At the same time as the two British midshipmen were having their discussion, Rear Admiral Nelson, having recovered from his debilitating injury sustained during the attempted invasion of Santa Cruz, was returning to Gibraltar. Following the invasion of Malta, the actual position and destination of the French Fleet was not known for definite, and Nelson had been ordered to find them and destroy them once and for all. His handwritten orders from the Admiralty would be far easier to read than actually carry out, but if one man could achieve the near impossible, it was Horatio Nelson. Obviously, the Rear Admiral's failure at San Cruz had been forgiven by those who directed his future.

Three days after John Pollard had learned of the rumours from Midshipman Smiley, HMS Vanguard, the Rear Admiral's current flagship, sailed into Gibraltar harbour, creating yet again, an atmosphere of anticipation amongst the warships at anchor there, beneath the safety of the British shore batteries.

After just a few days of planning and consultation with his captains, Nelson left, leading another small squadron, which did not include his friend, Sir Thomas Troubridge and HMS Culloden. Of course, the Culloden's crew were disappointed to have been left at anchor, and as consolation, their captain broke the traditional convention of the navy, not to allow seamen ashore when moored in a friendly harbour. It was a mistake, Troubridge was to later regret.

Gibraltar had been a British Overseas Territory for the past one hundred years or so, and sat on the southern tip of the Iberian Peninsula. A strip of land measuring three miles in length and one mile across. Its location on the border with Spain created exposure to an invasion by the Spanish, and for that reason, the colony was heavily fortified by cannon and troops.

Being such a limited land mass, the Culloden's crew were surprised by the number of refreshment and entertaining houses available to visit. The six midshipmen were also permitted to visit Gibraltar, and both Pollard and Smiley soon found themselves enjoying a walk through the busy streets, beneath the domineering Rock from which a multitude of cannon could be seen pointing out towards the Straits, in readiness to open fire on any enemy vessels that came within range.

Throughout that day they came across various crew members of their ship, taking full advantage of their temporary freedom by drinking and performing boisterously in a number of the many bars located in the town. Not far away from the celebrating seamen was the Boatswain, Mr. Grey, lingering and watching for any trouble that might erupt. Major Cuthbert, the officer in charge of the marines on HMS Culloden was also present ashore, with a number of his men strategically positioned to jump on any likelihood of confrontation.

"There's no doubt, both the Boatswain and Major are acting under instructions from the captain," Midshipman Smiley suggested, "Making certain there's no trouble."

"And I suspect to ensure our lads return to the ship before nightfall," Pollard added, "There's one thing Smiley that's been concerning me. During that last action at Santa Cruz, did you see Batson in any of the boats or on the beach?"

"No, I cannot say as I did. Mind you, after Nelson was shot, I was too involved in getting him back to the ship. Why do you ask?"

"I'm not sure, but I was one of the first to arrive back at Culloden, and I saw Baston standing on the poop deck, watching what was going on from afar."

"And you think he might have somehow, escaped any involvement in the attack?"

"Or could have hidden below somewhere when the boats were first launched, and without any of the other officers being aware he'd failed to leave the ship."

"That might explain the rumour that's been going around amongst the crew that he failed to do his duty. But it's a serious allegation to make without any proof that was the case."

"That's why I haven't mentioned anything until now."

"Well, I suggest we don't speak another word about it. After all, we're talking about cowardice in the face of the enemy, and you know what the penalty for that is?"

"Yes, of course."

The two Midshipmen entered a small bar on the main thoroughfare of Gibraltar, not that far from the border with Britain's enemy, Spain. They found the room to be crowded with mostly heavily intoxicated members of their ship's crew; some singing, others talking, but all of them in a noisy, celebratory mood.

Pollard purchased two glasses of local wine from a barman serving behind a wooden bench and pouring drinks from metal jugs. Not wanting to spoil the men's enjoyment, the two young officers managed to find a dark corner in which they sat and took a few gulps of the local beverage. It certainly felt good to escape from the confines of the ship and both men savoured the moment.

After a few minutes, they were surprised to see Midshipman Baston enter the bar in the company of another, younger officer, Midshipman Royston Crane. Amazingly, Baston was still grasping his rattan, which didn't go unnoticed by the others gathered inside.

"What in God's name is he doing carrying that cane in here?" Pollard quietly asked his friend and colleague, "Does he not realise he's only inviting trouble amongst the men?"

"Oh yes, I'm certain he does. That's why he's flashing it about in defiance of anybody who wishes to try and take it from him."

"I find it hard to believe that anyone could take so much pleasure in causing so much cruelty and grief to his fellow human beings."

"He knows only too well, his rank protects him from dishing out what punishment he chooses, and that the captain and their Lordships at the Admiralty would support him in whatever disciplinary action he took."

"There should be no place in the service for an individual such as that vagabond."

"I agree, wholeheartedly."

As the two men continued to discuss their fellow officer surreptitiously, and with both pairs of eyes fixed on the subject of their conversation, who was standing near to the wooden bench, drinking from a mug of ale, Joseph Cottonbill rose from his seat. The seaman and member of Culloden's crew was a larger than life individual whose black hair was tied in a knotted pigtail at the back. He appeared to be unsteady on his feet, and no one took much notice of him, until he made his way to the bar and stood facing Midshipman Batson. The man glared at the junior officer, with both large fists clenched at his side.

"This could be trouble," Smiley suggested, instantaneously standing from his chair.

The room fell silent, causing Mr. Batson to enquire what business

Seaman Cottonbill was about.

"Matty Brown was a shipmate of mine," the big man confirmed in a deep, slurred voice, with a broad Gloucestershire accent. His eyes were on fire, and Pollard assumed the man was one of many taken from the farms and pressed into service, not knowing a reef knot from a lanyard.

The youngest of the midshipmen quickly addressed two of the sailors sitting nearby and instructed them to take Joseph Cottonbill back to the ship immediately, in an attempt to avoid what appeared to be, inevitable. At first, they hesitated, not wanting to leave the drinking establishment, but then quickly realised it was an officer giving the order. As they also left their seats, the biggest man in the room was overheard to loudly announce, "Aye, and he was a better man than you, and was no coward."

"What are you suggesting mister?" Batson enquired, now grasping his cane at his side.

"You know exactly what I'm saying. You're nothing more than a bullying..."

The cane was rapidly raised above Batson's head and brought down in a ferocious arch, intending to split open the aggressor's face before more treasonous words could be spoken. But the arm wielding the birch was grabbed in mid-air, and the cane snatched from the midshipman's grasp.

"My God, you will pay for that," Batson threatened.

"In that case, I'd better make it worthwhile."

Cottonbill was already facing the death penalty having struck a King's officer, so in his drunken stupor, decided to go the whole hog, lashing the three-pronged rattan across Batson's face. The midshipman's features opened up like a ripened tomato, and blood began to pour down the front of his tunic.

Both the seamen ordered to take the drunken sailor back to the ship, grabbed an arm each, but were lifted from the floor like a couple of rag dolls, before being deposited across the room. A knife was produced, and Midshipman Pollard shouted out for the avenging seaman to cease forthwith.

Cottonbill turned his head and glared directly at John Pollard, shaking it and confessing, "This is for the good of all of my shipmates in the navy...sir." He then grabbed Mr. Batson's hair, and slit the midshipman's throat, causing the man to fall to the floorboards with more blood gushing out from an open, fatal wound. In his drunken stupor, and for whatever reason he could put forward to mitigate his action, it was a murder he had committed, and Seaman Cottonbill had just signed his own death warrant.

Pollard grabbed a metal jug of ale off the bar and crashed it down on top of the possessed seaman's head; once, twice, before Cottonbill finally collapsed to the floor.

Four red coated marines hurriedly entered the bar, pointing bayoneted rifles in front of them and causing Pollard to raise both arms, confirming the ruckus which had brought them there, was over. Realising the midshipman was an officer, they desisted from taking any further action. When he and Smiley crouched down over their fallen fellow officer, they found him to be as dead as a weevil squashed in a lump of stale bread.

The Boatswain was the next to enter the bar and immediately took charge, ordering the marines to take Seaman Cottonbill into custody, and return him back to the Culloden. In fact, every member of the crew was then ordered to return to the ship, which they did quietly and shocked by the event which had just taken place with such a sobering effect.

John Pollard took possession of the knife used by the killer and together with Smiley, arranged for the lifeless body of Henry Batson to be carried back to the launch awaiting their return. So much for an enjoyable festive day of free drinking and celebration.

Other captains were quickly summoned from their individual ships to assist with the trial on HMS Culloden. Although Sir Thomas Troubridge would never concede to having been mistaken by allowing his crew a day of drinking in Gibraltar, he must have appreciated that when the most detested officer on his ship faced the men, it was likely to spark the kind of disaster, which had taken place. But that would be no excuse for the doomed seaman who stood before the panel of captains.

Both Pollard and Smiley gave sworn evidence before Sir Thomas and the other senior officers, and Joseph Cottonbill was found guilty of murder most foul. He was inevitably sentenced to hang from the yardarm at dawn the following morning, in the presence of the entire ship's company.

No one really knew what thoughts went through the condemned prisoner's mind that night, as he sat in chains down in the hold, only that when he finally appeared on deck the following morning, he was grinning to himself. After being hoisted up with the rope tied around his neck, the giant of a man took a long time before his legs stopped twitching and the surgeon was finally able to pronounce death.

For days following the execution, the crew remained in a state of apathy and the officers went about their business sensitively. The only concern amongst the lieutenants and other officers, was that the whole affair could possibly spark mutinous behaviour. Alas, the remaining midshipmen broke with tradition, working hard to placate the crew members, until things began to get back to normal. During that uneasy period, discipline was maintained, but eventually Culloden was prepared to go to sea again without any further problem.

Midshipman Pollard played his part by working his cleaning detail hard, until the upper decks were once again, gleaming, much to the captain's delight. But Sir Thomas's delusionary blunder was never again to be repeated. The sooner he took his ship back out to sea, where each of his crewmen would become too busily worked to continue concentrating on the latest and final incident involving Midshipman Batson, the happier he would feel.

As a result of an incident involving the squadron of ships, which had earlier left Gibraltar with Rear Admiral Nelson, Captain Troubridge received new orders through the governor of Gibraltar. As the flotilla had approached Toulon in search of the French fleet, a severe gale had almost wrecked Nelson's flagship, HMS Vanguard, removing its topmasts and making it inoperable on the Corsican coast. The remainder of the ships of the line had been scattered by the severity of the same storm, and a number of frigates had been lost altogether. Those vessels, which had survived the fierce gale, sheltered at San Pietro Island, off Sardinia.

Midshipman Pollard was sent for by the captain and asked how much he knew about signalling aboard ship.

"Very little sir," the young officer answered, truthfully, and surprised by the question.

"Then Mr. Pollard, might I suggest you learn every detail there is to know about the employment. You have about a month to recognise every flag required."

"Might I respectfully ask, why sir?"

The captain was reluctant at first to explain further, but then told the midshipman that Culloden and other ships of the line would be soon supporting Rear Admiral Nelson near Toulon.

"You are to be transferred to HMS Vanguard as the Signal Midshipman, so get to it and quickly. And Mr. Pollard, not a word of what we have just spoken to anyone else in fear of your life; do you understand sir?"

"Aye, aye sir."

So, that was it. Midshipman Pollard was to become Nelson's Signal Midshipman, and the young man didn't know whether to rejoice at having been given such a position, or be afraid of what the future would hold. One thing was certain; under Nelson, he would be seeing more action than ever before. Also, he suspected the demons that had caused him so much personal discomfort in recent times, would not be returning in a hurry.

As the Culloden and ten other ships of the line left Gibraltar, heading for Toulon, First Lieutenant Johnson instructed Signal Midshipman Archibald Boulton to teach every flag involved in signalling to Mr. Pollard. Although, as ordered by the captain, the most recent student of naval signalling never spoke a word of his conversation with Captain Troubridge, Arthur Smiley guessed that something was about to happen, and it involved his friend and confidante.

The one piece of information it was found difficult to keep from the crew, was the details of the ship's destination. The rumour they were about to join Rear Admiral Nelson for yet another naval sortie, quickly spread around the 74-gun warship, and it was Midshipman Smiley who mentioned the subject to Pollard.

Both officers were below decks, resting following supper, when Smiley asked, "Will you be leaving the ship then, Pollard?"

"I cannot say," his friend confirmed.

Smiley looked hurt, but didn't press his enquiry.

Pollard was left feeling somewhat disturbed by the manner in which he'd just snubbed his colleague.

"Very well, Smiley, but what I am about to tell you, must go no further. You must give me your word."

Smiley nodded, relieved that his friend was about to take him into his confidence.

The younger officer explained his future, and the reason why he had been so energetically engaged with Culloden's Signalling Midshipman.

"My God John, you will be working directly to Nelson himself. How I envy you."

"I can only pray to God that Nelson enjoys more success than of late, during the time I'm aboard his ship."

They both laughed out aloud, attracting the attention of others who were just outside earshot.

Chapter Nine

By the time Captain Troubridge's fleet of ten ships of the line, together with a fourth-rate vessel met up with Nelson off Toulon, Midshipman Pollard had an excellent working knowledge of the numeric flag codes contained in the Admiralty's official Signal-Book. The young man was ready to transfer across to the Rear Admiral's flagship, HMS Vanguard, which by then had been hastily repaired and made sea worthy yet again.

After bidding farewell to Midshipman Smiley, he was taken across to his new berth by launch. In a strange way, Pollard was relieved to be leaving Culloden and all the sad memories behind him. In a short space of time, he had witnessed the murder of a fellow midshipman, no matter how justified that might have been, and the execution of a close shipmate, James McCreadie, which in his view had not been so justified. Of course, he would miss the companionship of Smiley, but his duty came above all else, and he boarded the Vanguard with a light heart.

She was a seventy-four-gunner, fully rigged with two gundecks and now, with the addition of eleven war ships, had sufficient support to pursue and intercept the French. The only problem still facing Nelson, was a lack of intelligence as to the location of the enemy. His difficulty was exacerbated by the absence of frigates to scout ahead of his newly supplemented squadron.

The first instruction given to Midshipman Pollard after his transfer to the flagship, was to signal to the fleet, 'All captains required to attend Vanguard'. That would of course include his old captain, Sir Thomas Troubridge. At first, the young man performed nervously when selecting the required flags to hoist up the main mast, and gained confidence when every vessel acknowledged. Soon after that first signal, the captains began to make their individual way to the Rear Admiral's flagship.

Nelson's Flag Captain was Edward Berry, a tall, slim man, always seen wearing a powdered wig. Thomas Bush was the First Lieutenant on Vanguard and George Antrim the Second Lieutenant. Mr. Ayde, a robust fellow with dark side whiskers down each side of his face, was the third Boatswain with whom Pollard had performed his duty. The traumatic memory of being tied across a cannon by Mr. Swann when serving on the Havik, and lashed across his exposed buttocks, had constantly remained with him. He would never forget the searing pain he suffered from that initial and only beating. Although Ayde didn't use his rattan as frequently as his predecessors, he constantly made his presence known by his loudly spoken voice, which frequently dispersed numerous metaphors when emphasising a point of view. Finally, the number of officers was made up by a complimentary group of five other midshipmen, as had been the case on the Culloden.

Lieutenant Antrim had made it quite clear that part of the new Signal Midshipman's responsibilities would be to remain close to the box containing the various signalling flags, except when being called upon by one of the officers. It was a suggestion Pollard didn't really need to be reminded of.

Captain Taddy was in charge of the marine force on board the flag ship; a proportionately built man with a straight back, grey hair and side whiskers. His constant posture was one of aggression, although in reality, he was the most affable of all the officers on board. It was Taddy who first noticed how nervous looking the new addition to the crew appeared to be. In a paternal way, the Captain of Marines took young Pollard to one side and explained that Rear Admiral Nelson was the very last man he needed to be concerned about.

"Aye laddie, His Lordship views every crew member as part of his family," the gentle giant of a Scotsman explained, "And believe me sonny, you will never have tasted meals like you will aboard the Vanguard. The Admiral believes that by feeding his men with proper heartily prepared meals, he will get the best out of them. Fresh fruit and vegetables are always on the daily roster." Captain Taddy noted a look of inquisitiveness on the young midshipman's face, and qualified his last remark by adding, "To prevent scurvy son. You'll not be finding any scurvy on any of the Admiral's ships."

"Oh, I see. That's good to know sir."

"Aye lad; mind you, he's no soft touch now. Many have made that misjudgement by believing him to be such, and have felt the cat on their backs soon enough. But answer the man honestly when he questions you, remain loyal to him, and you will find he's the fairest commander you have ever done your duty for."

"Yes, thank you sir."

Pollard appreciated the character profile relayed to him by the Captain of Marines, and from that day onwards, continued performing with confidence and all the dedication he could muster. Taddy's words concerning the food on board were soon proved to be right, when the midshipman tasted his first salted beef with rice and vegetables, and plenty of it, served on a wooden square shaped plate. The fact that the men always appeared to be jovial and in good spirits supported Nelson's philosophy.

Following that first meeting with his captains, the Vice Admiral moved his squadron southwards and stopped at Naples, where the British Ambassador, Sir William Hamilton informed him that the French fleet had already passed Sicily, heading for Malta. That was the first occasion

Nelson met Lady Hamilton, Sir William's wife and his future lover.

The Rear Admiral took the unusual step of asking King Ferdinand of Naples if he could borrow the King's frigates to assist in scouting for the French. Unfortunately, His Majesty refused in fear of reprisals from Napoleon, so the British had to continue their vain search by using ships of the line as forward positioning scouts. How Nelson wished for the speed and agility of frigates, their absence thus making his immediate task slow and frustrating.

As the fleet slowly made its way through the Mediterranean, John Pollard had the strangest feeling that, having served for some time at sea, he had returned home, as if he was back in the heart of England. Everywhere he visited and observed on the Vanguard, appeared to have Nelson's influence.

The Culloden had always been a busy ship, particularly during daylight hours, but Vanguard was more industrious. Those crew members, when on duty, appeared to be always going about their business with more purpose, constantly working on the rigging, trimming sails, cleaning the decks below, and running out the guns before bringing them back in again, and most of the activities being timed against the clock. There seemed to be more enthusiasm and deliberation about the hands, and the midshipman remembered the words of Captain Taddy when he explained that Nelson believed his men worked much harder on full stomachs, and when in the best of health. It seemed to be common sense to the new addition, and he wondered why other captains didn't follow the Rear Admiral's lead. In any case, Midshipman Pollard now realised why so many of the hardened and experienced sailors queued up to sail under the man, who it seemed all of England adored and looked towards in times of crisis.

The first time the young man set eyes on the most famous sailor of them all, was one late afternoon when the Rear Admiral appeared on the poop deck with his flag captain and First Lieutenant. Unexpectedly, he suddenly called for his Signal Midshipman.

Pollard leapt on to the deck and stood facing the great man, noticing the patch over his one eye, made mention of by Arthur Smiley at Santa Cruz, and the armless sleeve of his jacket.

Nelson smiled at him and said, "Ah, is it not Troubridge's signal man, I fear I purloined from my old and trusted friend."

"Aye, aye sir," Pollard answered, sheepishly, and raising a couple of closed knuckles to his forehead in salute.

Both the captain and lieutenant smiled at the young figure standing there, confirming the small group of officers were extremely affable and obviously proud to be serving under the celebrated Rear Admiral.

"Welcome aboard young sir."

"Thank you, sir."

"Signal, Flag to the fleet, remain in close formation, if you please Mr.

Pollard. I need my ships to be closer to me."

The young midshipman felt immediately invigorated when realising the commander actually knew his name.

"Aye, aye sir, the fleet is to remain in close formation."

The young officer felt as though all the eyes on that poop deck were watching, as he hurriedly selected the appropriate numbered flags from his box and hoisted them up for the fleet to see. He then stood on the quarterdeck examining each accompanying ship of the line through his telescope, before returning to the Rear Admiral.

"All ships have acknowledged sir," he announced.

"Yes, thank you."

It was precisely at that moment, as Pollard was returning to the quarterdeck to await further instructions, a voice bellowed from up high in the crow's nest, "To the deck, ship ho, on the starboard bow sir."

"Colours Mr. Seymour?" Captain Berry shouted back.

"She's one of ours, sir; a brig with two square-rigged masts, heading directly for us."

Within a few minutes, the sails of the other vessel could be seen from the Vanguard's decks, and all eyes were looking in her direction.

"To the deck," the same lookout called out, "She's sending a boat to us sir."

"It's the Neptune sir, out of Ragusa I believe," Captain Berry confirmed.

The small boat came alongside, and a smartly dressed young lieutenant appeared on the deck, before saluting the Vanguard's Second Lieutenant, George Antrim, there to greet the visiting officer. After a few words of welcome were exchanged, the messenger from Neptune was escorted by Mr. Antrim to the Rear Admiral.

"With the compliments of Captain Sanders of HMS Neptune sir," the visitor announced, before handing a sealed envelope to Nelson, who, rather than seeking the privacy of his cabin to read the contents, broke the seal and opened the enclosure there and then.

Nelson carefully scrutinised the missive, before thanking the lieutenant, indicating there would be no reply, and suggesting the officer should return to the brig. He then once again, called for his Signal Midshipman.

"If you please Mr. Pollard, Flag to the fleet, all captains to the Flag," he instructed the young officer, this time, with a more serious tone to his voice.

"Aye, aye sir, all captains to the Flag."

What followed that signal was a lengthy meeting in Nelson's cabin with his captains, and the contents of the message delivered by Neptune, soon became known to the other officers on the flagship. It had been confirmed that the French convoy had sailed from Malta just a week previously, heading eastwards from the Greek island. It was decided that Egypt was the next target, and Nelson immediately directed Captain Berry to set a course for Alexandria.

During the Dog Watch following the meeting with the captains, who by then had all returned to their ships, men continued to work on the sails, maintaining maximum advantage of a stiff westerly breeze coming off the landfall. And yet, with all the various activities ongoing, a strange silence enveloped the ship, one that Midshipman Pollard had never experienced before. Only later, did the junior officer learn that Nelson insisted the crew went about their duties quietly and with the least possible fuss, especially at times when he was in his cabin.

As the last flickers of the sun disappeared beyond the horizon, Nelson remained in the isolation of his retreat. Knowing he would not be required at that particular moment, Pollard stood on the stern rail in self-absorption, as had always been his practice at that time when day was turning into night. Watching the ripples of a calm sea striking the side of the ship, he was beginning to miss the company of his old friend, Arthur Smiley. Somewhere close by, in the darkness of the hour, Culloden was at anchor, and he wondered what his fellow midshipman would be doing at that very moment. He smiled to himself, thinking of the courageous manner in which his one-armed colleague energetically covered the decks, bellowing out his orders and refusing to allow any idling amongst the crew.

He then began to wonder how things were back at home with his father and sister. Whilst the utmost enthusiasm and speculation continued to run through the ship, the young midshipman couldn't help but feel somewhat melancholic. Finally, knowing there would be no further signals sent from the flagship that night, Pollard retired to his hammock below decks, with the roll of the Vanguard helping him to sleep. Little did he, or any other member of the ship's crew, know that the British fleet was passing the unseen French position. Even Rear Admiral Nelson was unaware of the close encounter, beneath the cloak of darkness.

In their haste to reach Alexandria as soon as possible, the British had unwittingly passed the French convoy during that same night, therefore reaching their destination before the enemy. Surprised to find their prey absent, the search continued, and Nelson led his fleet on a north by north east bearing, reaching the Anatolia coast a few days later. Still, there was no sign of the elusive French ships, so the Rear Admiral decided to return to Sicily in the hope of coming across the enemy fleet, as Vanguard made way, followed by the remainder of the fleet.

Shortly after that close encounter, those who Nelson was seeking, finally reached Alexandria, and Napoleon landed his army, which stormed the Egyptian city successfully, before moving further inland to secure a tight foothold on the surrounding countryside.

The absence of frigates to scout the waters ahead of the main flotilla, continued to hamper the search. Nelson's progress was sluggish and painstaking, and he could only assume the enemy vessels were somewhere in the eastern Mediterranean. After resupplying his ships, he once again left Syracuse in Sicily and headed in that direction. Finally, two ships, HMS Alexander and HMS Swiftsure, sighted the French squadron at Alexandria, following two months of sailing through the Mediterranean without success.

The British had found its quarry, and amongst a re-invigorated crew, the drums rolled and the pursuers cleared for action. Midshipman Pollard had seen it all before, but perhaps not so efficiently or as quickly enacted. On this occasion, as the British approached the line of enemy ships, there was no meeting of the captains. Each of them knew fully what was expected of them and the ships under their control, although, under Nelson's orders, the Signal Midshipman was constantly turning to his Signal-Book and sending messages from the flag ship to the rest of the fleet.

The commander of the enemy vessels, Vice-Admiral Brueys, had placed his ships in what he believed was a formidable defensive position, and which the British commander scrutinised from a distance. After studying the French dispositions, the order to attack immediately was given, via Midshipman Pollard. As the Vanguard rolled forward, with its bow dipping and rising to the waves, the advancement of the British fleet began.

Nelson's ships split into two divisions, one cutting across the head of the enemy's line, and passing between the cabled French and the shoreline. Cables replacing anchors, allowed vessels to turn their broadsides in any direction, as the British ships approached. Nelson's second division had been ordered to engage the enemy on the seaward side in an attempt to catch the enemy in a crossfire. As soon as the advanced ships came within range, the cannons roared and for three hours, Midshipman Pollard watched from where he stood, close to Nelson's side. It was a re-enactment of the vision he frequently had when a mere child of tender years, only now, in reality, there were no French snipers to contend with.

Initially, the centre of the French line managed to repel the British attack, and again the Rear Admiral turned to his Signal Midshipman to order reinforcements for the attack to be renewed. Ships acknowledged as they focused on the strongest point of the French defence. Then as night came, and the battle continued, Pollard gasped as he saw Brueys flagship, Orient, unexpectedly explode, lighting up the Egyptian coastline with flames reaching skywards.

The centre of the line of defence had been defeated, and with their commander dead, the back line of the French fleet attempted to break out of the bay.

Vanguard's heavy guns came back into play and a veil of black smoke enveloped the ship, as she pounded the sides of the fleeing ships with broadside after broadside.

Midshipman Pollard heard the Rear Admiral suddenly cry out, and turned to see Nelson had been hit above his right eye by a fragment of shot.

Both Captain Berry and Lieutenant Bush ran to his assistance and for a short time, it appeared Nelson had been mortally wounded.

"I am killed," he was overheard to say, "Remember me to my wife."

Pollard and the others were shocked that their leader's announcement might be true, but although continuing to bleed profusely, pale and concussed, the stricken commander remained at his post to continue with the battle.

The enemy fleet was pummelled into defeat and victory was Nelson's to claim. From a total of seventeen warships, only two French ships of the line and two frigates escaped the carnage. Every British ship resounded in loud cheers, and men danced a victory jig, until being reminded of the need to remain disciplined by their officers.

The Rear Admiral looked down into the blackened face of his Signal Midshipman and just smiled. There was blood on Nelson's face and staining the side of his neck; but it mattered not. Britain's most successful fighting naval commander had finally gained another long-awaited victory. The whole of Britain would celebrate, and Pollard wondered what the reaction of his father and sister would be, when they received the news.

Unfortunately, as HMS Vanguard was leaving the Egyptian coastline for Naples, Nelson came down with a fever, complaining that his head was 'splitting, splitting, splitting'. By the time the flag ship anchored to allow repairs to be made to minor damage to the vessel, the Rear Admiral decided he would use Naples as a stop-over, to recover from his head injury and bout of fever.

He was well cared for by Sir William and Lady Hamilton during his stay in Naples. At the same time, John Pollard, together with the other officers and crew members, managed to get some respite from the arduous demands of maintaining a ship of the line, although daily duties continued in a celebratory mood. What had been a thrilling and exhilarating strategically run battle, was now replaced by the rewards of victory. All on board hoped the same warm and glorious welcome Vanguard received from the people on the south west coast of the Italian peninsula, would be repeated when they eventually returned to England.

That would never be in doubt, as unknown to any of them, all of the country was talking about the latest victory imposed on the French fleet by their naval hero. The streets of Portsmouth were already being decorated by bunting, in preparation for a warm welcome home for Horatio Nelson and his brave mariners.

Chapter Ten

The near destruction of the French fleet just off Alexandria, by the British warships, earned its place in history, commonly referred to as the Battle of the Nile. Dated records would show however, the success of Nelson's victory had far more severe repercussions for the French Emperor, Napoleon Bonaparte, that went far beyond the removal of any threat imposed by his decimated fleet. The marked triumph turned the confrontational situation between France and Britain dramatically in the latter's favour. With his army trapped in Egypt and the Royal Navy having control over the Syrian coast, other European nations began to turn against the French. The defeat of Napoleon's Mediterranean fleet had proved costly. His was a helpless and hopeless position, and whilst the once dictator of the majority of the continent, was busy dealing with the latest threat to his Empire, the victor was returning home to England; to a hero's welcome.

News of the French defeat had reached the mother country well in advance of the flagship HMS Vanguard approaching Portsmouth harbour. Cheering crowds were on the quayside as the vessel could be seen anchoring in the short distance, with its crew waving back in response. It was indeed, a new experience for the youngest officer on board, and Midshipman Pollard stood at the side of the other officers acknowledging the waving flags, in awe of the triumphant scenes. Only then, as he felt goose pimples rising from his neck upwards, did he realise it had been four years since the young man had last set foot on dry land, except of course for that distressing one day in Gibraltar and the skirmishes at Santa Cruz. But now, his only thoughts and ambitions were to see his father and sister, guessing that Rose would now be a young lady.

The crew had done their honourable duty and was to be paid off, but Nelson had made a personal point of confirming that the devotion to duty displayed by his Signal Midshipman, had not gone unnoticed. The Rear Admiral hoped the young man would serve with him again in the near future. Midshipman Pollard thanked and saluted the country's hero, before disembarking and seeking out a carriage to transport him to Plymouth. That particular search was not difficult, and he was thrilled by the compliments and pats on the back, received as he made his way to a line of carriages waiting to take England's most recent heroes to where ever they required, free of charge.

The welcoming weather was glorious with a springtime cloudless sky turning the country into a picturesque scene of beauty and joy. How different it all was from the rolling waves and grey skies confronted during the return voyage northwards through the Bay of Biscay. Away from the celebratory hubbub, the former Signal Midshipman sat back enjoying the peace and quiet of the countryside, as the coach rattled its way across the rural scenery. The driver had already congratulated the young man, pumping his hand as if it was to be his last day on earth, and now he was alone with only his own self to keep him company, relishing the serenity that surrounded him. Free to focus on his own thoughts and no longer being a single cog in a massive machine of human endeavour.

Young Pollard had forgotten just how impressionable the rolling hills, green fields and hedgerows were at this time of year, and surprisingly found himself becoming more desperate to arrive home, the closer he got to Plymouth. How he was longing for those evenings in front of a log fire, sharing his tales of adventure and hardship with his father and sister. Already, the rolling movement of the ship; the noise of men scrubbing decks; climbing the rigging and running out the guns, seemed to have been left in the far distant past.

With his sack carried across his back, he quickly made his way up the narrow-cobbled streets from the harbour. Apart from the glances and smiles afforded the young man in naval uniform, from people passing by, nothing seemed to have changed. The horse and carts were still dominant;

the smell of freshly baked bread still lingered in the air, and young urchins playing amongst the horse manure, were still there, as boisterous as before.

When he finally reached his father's terraced house, he somehow felt as if he was a stranger, seeking lodgings. After being away for such a lengthy period of time, he certainly didn't feel like a returning prodigal, and began to wonder about the reception he was about to receive. Deep down though, he knew his concerns were baseless, but couldn't avoid wondering in what manner he would be greeted, if at all. He placed his sack of belongings on the step, and straightened to adjust his uniform jacket, the same one his father had made for him all those years before. He coughed to clear his throat, and after taking a deep breath, knocked on the door with more than a little apprehension.

At first, there was no answer, so he knocked again, only louder. When the door finally opened, he hardly recognised the attractive young lady standing there. She was tall and slim, radiating elegance with her dark brown hair tied up at the nape of her neck. She was beautiful, wearing a patterned dress of small red flowers, which complimented the complexion of her face.

"I don't believe it," she said, staring at him with her dark hazel eyes, "John, you've come home." Her posture was different. She looked and spoke like an adult, much to his amazement.

It was Rose, and for a moment her brother just stood motionless and bemused by the apparition before him.

"Might I be allowed inside, Rose?" he humorously remarked.

"Only if you are intent on staying young sir," she answered with a warm smile, and mocking him by curtseying.

They both laughed and hugged each other with all the love, only a sister and brother could bestow on each other.

She showed him through to the kitchen at the back of the small house, and promised to make him some tea.

"You must be famished and thirsty John. It is so good to see you."

"And you Rose, but what happened to that mischievous little sister I once knew?"

"She grew up," Rose answered, indicating a wooden stool for him to sit on, and putting a light to a kettle resting on a hob that was standing in the corner near to a small window. The smell of cooked meat told the visitor, a meal had recently been prepared and probably devoured.

"Where's father, I so much want to see him again?" he enquired.

The expression on the young lady's face quickly changed to one more solemn, bringing some concern to her brother.

"He's upstairs in bed, John. I'm afraid father has the consumption and has been confined to his room for the past two weeks now. The apothecary says he must rest, but that's all he can do. He eats very little and drinks even less."

Without saying another word, the draper's son stood and quickly made his way up the bare wooden staircase on to the landing above. He found his father lying with his eyes closed, beneath his sheets and with both frail looking arms resting on the top. One hand was grasping a bloodstained piece of rag, and the window was partially opened, allowing the small room to be filled with the noises from the street outside.

John stood over him, looking sorrowfully down at his stricken father, remembering a time long ago, when Thomas Pollard would be out of his bed at four o'clock every morning, to drive his horse and cart when delivering bales of cloth around the district. The young man quickly recalled those visits to the naval dockyard at Devonport, where his ambitions towards a future life at sea were a mere embryo to be later developed into reality.

The elderly man suddenly coughed, and held the rag to his mouth, before opening his tired eyes and staring up at the figure standing over him.

"John?" he gasped.

"Yes father, I'm home."

"Thank God." His father then entered into a severe coughing fit, as Rose entered the room and lifted the suffering man's head off the pillow, before holding a glass of water to his mouth.

Thomas took a few sips, and then became more stable, lying back with both eyes transfixed on his son.

"I take it you are in fine health?" he asked in a croaking voice, his eyes searching, as if looking for a missing limb, or worse.

"Yes father, but distressed to find you so disabled and in need of help."

"It's nothing. The apothecary tells me I should be back on my feet within a few days John," the old man lied, "How long will you be staying with us?"

"Long enough father, but there's much to do, and I need to help Rose nurse you, until you are well enough again."

A slight smile interrupted the grey solemn face, and Thomas insisted, "You must tell us everything about what's happened to you, John."

"I will father, I promise." The old man turned to his daughter and remarked, "Doesn't he look well Rose? What did I tell you girl, your brother is a survivor."

"Yes, but now father," Rose quietly spoke, "You must rest, and I shall bring John back up to see you again a little later."

The old man's watery eyes closed and he sank back into oblivion, after whispering, "God bless all in this house. My son has returned safe."

Dusk was falling quickly, as brother and sister revisited a favourite location overlooking Plymouth's harbour, where they used to go when much younger and well before John Pollard first went off to sea. It seemed to the young midshipman that those glorious visits belonged to another previous life, as if he'd been transported off to another world and had only just returned.

They both sat beside each other on a small wooden bench, holding hands and admiring the view below them with sentimental thoughts of a time long ago. All was well and he was happy to be home, away from the arduous tasks of surviving at sea. It was John who interrupted their reverie. "Has the apothecary given you any idea how much longer father has left, Rose?" he enquired softly, looking across the harbour at the gathering of numerous sailing vessels, and knowing his sister would answer truthfully.

"No, he hasn't said, but I fear he cannot hold out for much longer. He seems to have coughed up more blood than he drinks water. How has life been treating you, John? Were you involved in any battles? Father is always demanding I read to him the news about the ongoing war with France, especially any information appertaining to confrontations involving our navy."

"Have you managed to tell him about the most recent battle off the Egyptian coast Rose?"

"Of course, John, they are calling it the Battle of the Nile, Admiral Nelson's greatest victory yet. The whole of the country has been in celebration from what I can make out." The young lady paused, as if suddenly realising something important. She then coyly asked, "Were you there, John?"

"Yes sister, I was there. I served as Nelson's Signal Midshipman on the Vanguard. It was a great honour."

"My God John, you must tell father all about it. What kind of man is he?"

"Who, father?"

She laughed. "Stop teasing, you know who I mean; Admiral Nelson."

"Everything they write about him Rose is true. He's a brave and courageous leader who persists in whatever duty is given him. There's no one better, or as good, believe me. But let's go back home, and I will tell you and father all about it."

The remainder of that evening was spent by the two siblings sitting at their father's candle lit bedside, with John describing to Thomas Pollard, all that had taken place at Alexandria, including the injury sustained by Nelson whilst on board the Vanguard. He refrained from making any mention of the fiasco experienced at Santa Cruz, or of the grotesque injuries suffered by many of the crews during the battle. Of the blood and loss of limbs: the screams and groans as men fell beneath the enemy's cannon.

His father said very little during his son's oration, but listened to every word intently, occasionally smiling when John described the routing of the French fleet.

"It's no wonder all England is celebrating John," he finally whispered, "You must be feeling extremely proud of your commander, as proud as I am of your own achievements."

"Thank you, father, but all I did was relay the orders of the Admiral to the rest of the fleet during the action."

"And yet, we would not have succeeded if those orders had not been sent or received."

Thomas held out an open hand, with some difficulty, and his son grasped it.

"How your mother would have been so proud if she'd have been here this day." The stricken man then lay back his head and closed his eyes yet again, after Rose had made him drink more water from a glass permanently at the side of his bed. She told her brother that their father must now rest for the remainder of the night, and that she had warmed John's bed for him, in his old room. How different it was when he lay on his old mattress, without constantly feeling the movement of the ship; his ears picking up every sound of the watch working above his head.

The following morning, the young midshipman visited his mother's grave, where he spent most of that day, praying and telling his beloved mother all about his life's experiences. He was still feeling her loss and fretted on the possibility that he was also about to lose his father.

When he finally straightened in readiness to leave, having suddenly realised how quickly the time had passed by, he turned to see his sister Rose standing waiting for him. Her face was pale, and she had tears in her eyes. Her brother realised immediately what had happened.

"Father has gone John," she mournfully said, "I sent for the apothecary but it was too late and he passed away peacefully. But before he died, he asked for you, and I told him you were with mother."

The young lady's brother took the news of his father's demise harshly, weeping as he escorted his younger sister back to their home. Although he'd spent the last four years away from Plymouth, he'd always loved and admired the man who had managed to raise both his children alone, and would always be thankful for his father's efforts and commitment towards the two of them.

Thomas Pollard was laid to rest next to his wife, and following the graveside service, John and Rose left the cemetery holding hands, both bound together by their grief. The young naval officer enquired about what his sister intended to do, now she would be alone in their father's house.

"Fear not for me John, I shall live with Mr. and Mrs. Simpson at the Dog and Doublet. They have been very supportive and have offered to afford me a room there."

"So, you shall be selling father's house?"

"Yes, I think it's best John, there are too many uncomfortable memories there, but I shall place half of the amount I receive in an account in your name, if you are agreeable."

"No Rose, I do not wish you to do that. I earnestly want you to keep the total amount of father's estate. You have earned it and although a midshipman's pay isn't a great deal, it is sufficient for my needs."

His sister argued but John Pollard was adamant.

As the days passed by, following the funeral, although the emotions resulting from the death of his father were still raw, he managed to turn his mind back to his naval career, wondering when the call would be received ordering his return to service. It seemed so long ago now, when he was last at sea, and yet he had only been ashore for no longer than a couple of weeks. Of course, he was thankful his father had lived to witness his return, but John's life could never be the same again. Apart from his sister, there was no one else left to impress; to boast to about various achievements and to make proud. The hollowness he was feeling inside would remain for a long time to come.

Early each morning, he undertook a stroll through the town, and would spend a little time observing the busy harbour from a vantage point. It was by sheer coincidence that during one of his walks, with his thoughts concentrating on memories of life on board the Vanguard, a familiar figure suddenly appeared, walking towards him on the opposite side of the narrow lane. John had to look twice initially, but yes; it was most definitely him. In the living flesh, his old and most trusted one-armed friend was ambling towards him.

"Arthur," he called out, "You old sea dog."

Both men embraced each other in the middle of the thoroughfare and Midshipman Smiley quickly explained he was about to call on his old friend, his ship having anchored off Portsmouth.

After congratulating each other on how well they looked, Smiley enquired, "Have you not heard who is here present in Plymouth?"

Pollard shook his head, looking at his friend inquisitively.

"Nelson; Admiral Nelson is to be given the freedom of Plymouth in recognition of his victory at the Battle of the Nile."

"That's wonderful news Smiley, but what brings you to Plymouth, pray tell?"

"I've been transferred to the St George, John. She's Nelson's new ship and word has it we are about to sail to the Baltic."

Of course, the younger of the two was pleased for his friend, but couldn't avoid feeling a little dejected, not having been summoned for duty on the same flag ship.

"I was sorry to hear about your father John, and was coming to visit to give you my condolences."

"Thank you, that is a kind gesture, but come back with me and I shall introduce you to Rose, my sister."

Smiley reminded his friend of the time he had visited both Pollard's father and sister, shortly after having his arm removed on the Culloden. His friend was pleased that he had met his father whilst still alive.

It was fortuitous that on the same day Midshipman Pollard was reunited with his old friend and colleague, when he returned to his father's house, a letter was awaiting his attention. It was from the Admiralty, signed by Horatio Nelson, now Vice Admiral, instructing the officer to report forthwith to HMS St George at Portsmouth. He was to take up his former position of Signal Midshipman, yet again. The young man received the news with mixed emotions. Obviously, he was happy at having been selected to serve under Nelson for a second time, but on this occasion, his father wouldn't be there to give his blessings and see him off.

"Are you not pleased Pollard with the order?" Smiley enquired, noticing a look of indifference on his friend's face.

"Of course, but the last time I was summoned by a letter from the Admiralty, I was promoted to midshipman. I thought at least I would have made lieutenant on this occasion."

Both of them laughed together, with Rose happy to see her brother's humour had finally returned.

Chapter Eleven

The ongoing preparations for going to sea was intense on HMS St George. Amongst the daily activities, there was a constant line of supply ships bringing various requested and necessary requisitions. She was without doubt, one of the most potent fighting ships in the fleet; a Duke-class ship of the line carrying eight hundred and fifty souls. The St George's armament consisted of a total of ninety-eight guns and she was fully rigged.

By now, Midshipman Pollard was used to hanging his hammock on a strange vessel, and quickly became fully acquainted with his new fellow officers and surroundings. He was certainly made to feel welcome by the captain, Thomas Hardy, an extremely tall man with a reputation for being amicable and caring towards his crew. The fact that the man in charge of the ship had previously served under Nelson was telling, and in similar fashion to the Vice Admiral, constantly showed a willingness to genuinely care for the welfare of his men.

Albeit, Pollard was a junior officer on the St George, there seemed to lack the disciplinary cutting edge experienced in previous berths. Such a constant appeared to have been replaced with greater respect for rank, securing the relationship between senior and subordinate members of the crew, although of course, the overall effect of naval supervision and orderliness remained. Flogging and birching were still a threat to those who wished to challenge authority.

News that the Fleet Commander was about to embark lifted hearts and souls, and when Nelson was finally piped aboard his new flagship, both midshipmen Pollard and Smiley watched with enthusiasm the short ceremony, as the navy's most respected individual acknowledged the salutes. It was the first time the two young men had stood together in service since their time spent on HMS Culloden, and both felt tremendous pride, as Nelson was escorted to his cabin by the smiling and respectful Captain Hardy.

Within just two days of Pollard joining Nelson's new flagship, the ongoing work to make her ready for sea was completed. Without further delay, she left Portsmouth to stand off Great Yarmouth at one of the Royal Navy's strategic east coast anchorage points at Yarmouth Roads. In the days that followed, little was seen of Nelson, the Vice Admiral being engaged in planning and discussions with many of his senior officers. Occasionally, he would appear on deck, look at those ships already close by, as if counting them, and then disappear back to his maps and records kept in his cabin.

Both Pollard and Smiley watched with interest as other ships of the line appeared and anchored close to the St George.

"You know I told you back in Plymouth, it had been rumoured we were going to the Baltic, Pollard?" Midshipman Smiley recalled.

"I remember."

"Well, I was talking with the Second Lieutenant, Mr. Place, only this morning and he confirmed that's exactly where we are going." Arthur Smiley was like a ferret amongst the officers of whatever ship he served on, gleaning snippets of information and wallowing in a position where he knew more than most of the other members of the crew, and on occasions, other officers.

"According to Mr. Place, the powers that be have become concerned about a group of ships he called, the League of Armed Neutrality, led by Russia with Denmark, Sweden and Prussia involved."

"You mean we are going to war with all of those countries?"

Midshipman Smiley shook his head. "Apparently, this league is trying to enforce free trade with France and has been threatening the British blockade up there in the Baltic. Again, according to Mr. Place, its existence also threatens the important supply of timber from Scandinavia to England, and the politicians are not very happy about it; neither are the

Lords of the Admiralty."

"So that's what this is all about? Nelson is putting together a fleet to attack this so-called Russian led league? My God Smiley, I suspect we shall need one hell of a lot of ships to pull that off, don't you think?"

"It very much seems like it, my old friend." Smiley sat back, grinning like a cat that had just got the cream, happy that he had once again, been one step in front of his shipmates when soliciting intelligence usually restricted to the senior officers on a ship, and in many cases, just the captain. Whether the older midshipman's information had been accurate, was yet to be seen, but when Nelson was first sighted on the quarter deck in the presence of Hardy, he appeared to be impatient and frustrated. He turned to his Signal Midshipman and instructed, "Mr. Pollard, it's a pleasure to see you again. Please signal, flag to the fleet, God save the King, if you please."

"Aye, aye sir, God save the King."

"What in the Devil's name, is he waiting for," Nelson was then overheard to say to his fleet captain, obviously referring to Admiral Hyde Parker, who was in overall command of the squadron now gathered in totality, off Great Yarmouth.

Pollard couldn't quite catch Hardy's reply, as he quickly made his way to the quarterdeck to select the necessary flags to hoist up the St George's main mast.

"Thomas, it stands to reason, the time to strike is now," Nelson continued, slapping the side of his thigh with his one arm, "Once the Baltic thaw comes about, the Russians will be able to release their ships from Kronstadtg and Reval."

"That sir will number the opposing ships to well over a hundred," Hardy remarked, "A formidable force indeed, if I might say."

The commander looked up at his captain with concern, as if that was the first time such news had reached him, but already knowing the kind of opposition he could be facing. He then stormed off, back to his cabin. Unknown to everyone else on board, the impatient Vice Admiral wrote a letter to his old friend Captain Thomas Troubridge of the Culloden, who was then a Lord Commissioner of the Admiralty, complaining of the delay. Quickly following that private note, orders were sent to Admiral Parker suggesting the fleet should sail immediately for Copenhagen. The purpose of the reiterated orders was to detach the Danes from the League, earlier mentioned by Midshipman Smiley to Pollard, either by amicable agreement or hostilities if necessary. The British fleet was then to vigorously attack the Russians at Reval and Kronstadt, the object being to unsettle the Russians and eventually make their aggressive league ineffective.

Warm coats and sou'westers were the clothing of the day, as the fleet, led by Parker, sailed northwards towards the hostile weather conditions of the Baltic. Midshipman Pollard's work really began in earnest during that initial voyage, signals being constantly sent between the flagship and other ships of the line. Meetings became an everyday occurrence between Nelson and the captains, with the occasional updates being relayed to Admiral Parker.

When the British fleet reached the Skaw, they were met by a British diplomat, Nicholas Vansittart. The King's representative in Scandinavia confirmed that Denmark had rejected an ultimatum to ally itself with Britain, although neither Parker or Nelson had any knowledge of such a demand having been sent. They could only assume the threat had been sourced by the diplomatic service.

An overdue meeting took place between the two men in charge of the British ships, with Parker wanting to blockade the Baltic. Nelson however, pointed out the folly of creating more delay, and persuaded the Admiral to attack the Danish fleet concentrated off Copenhagen. He was still impatient to deal with the Danes before the Russians could set sail and organise themselves and the Swedes, before coming to Denmark's assistance.

A signal was sent to the rest of the fleet, via Midshipman Pollard, to keep in tight formation, as they passed through the narrows between Denmark and Sweden, attempting to remain as far away from the Danish guns as possible. In doing so, they were exposed to the Swedish batteries, but fortunately they stayed silent. However, the problems facing the fleet involved the lack of charts or pilots, requiring Captain Hardy to take soundings in the channel leading up to the Danish line, and having to work throughout the night. It was virtually impossible to discover the deepest part of the channel, and the would-be attackers had to remain far to seaward, relying on the Swedes reluctance to use their fire power.

The Danes had prepared well, positioning vessels not fitted for sea along the shore but still heavily armed, and supported by forts having sixty-eight guns, the equivalent of any ship of the line. In the entrance to Copenhagen harbour, Nelson and his senior officers noticed there were two ships of the line, a large frigate and two brigs, all rigged for sea, together with two immobile hulks. The Vice Admiral failed to recognise any threat represented by the Danish defence line. However, he was concerned about other supporting features, which could be seen from the flag ship. There were a number of shore batteries covering the water between the Danish line and shore. Also, further out to sea was a large shoal constricting the channel and endangering ships which might get too close and run aground.

Admiral Parker decided to remain with his heavier ships, which were incapable of entering the shallows of the channel, and would deal with any external interference from the Swedes or Russians. At this point, Nelson moved his flag from the St George to a shallower ship of the line, HMS

Elephant, to gain access and progress further up the channel. He took with him twelve other ships of the line with the shallowest drafts, together with some of the smaller vessels in the fleet.

Midshipman Smiley was ordered to remain on board the St George, and John Pollard transferred across to the Elephant, taking with him his box of flags necessary for communicating with the remainder of the fleet.

During the evening preceding the intended attack, Nelson met once again with his senior officers on board his new flagship and considered a number of obstacles, which would have to be overcome if success was to be achieved. The greatest problem facing the British were the fixed batteries protecting the harbour, which had a significant advantage over ship borne cannon because of their greater stability and bigger guns. Also, it was possible the Danes could reinforce their ships during battle, even though they were mostly small and would be out gunned by the whole of Nelson's force.

Finally, the Vice Admiral decided on a one to one confrontation, whereby his ships would approach the weaker, southern end of the Danish defences, in a line parallel with the enemy. The foremost ship would draw alongside a Danish vessel and anchor, before engaging that ship. The following line of British vessels would pass outside that ongoing engagement, until meeting the next Danish ship and repeat the same manoeuvre, until each ship in the Danish line had been dealt with in that fashion. It was a strategy welcomed and regarded by each of the captains as being the kind of precocious plan, which could bring the confrontation to an early end in favour of the British fleet, if all went as well as they hoped.

At the same time as the main part of the force were engaging the enemy, the frigate HMS Desiree, together with the smaller gun brigs, would rake the Danish line from the south, and a force led by Captain Edward Riou of HMS Amazon, would attack the northern end of the enemy line. Once the Danish opposition had been subdued, marines would be landed to attack the defending fortress. After those Danish ships at the southern end of the defending line had been disabled, bomb vessels could be brought closer to shore to threaten Copenhagen itself, and pave the way for negotiations to take place with Nelson having the upper hand.

It was a daring and remarkable plan devised by Nelson, but like all well intended strategies, it had to be executed with precision and complete understanding. Midshipman Pollard wasn't the only one impressed by the Vice Admiral's idea, and the meeting broke up with some officers confident it could be successfully executed. As was the usual case, there were others who were not so confident, and only time would decide the inevitable success, or failure.

With a southerly wind to assist, Nelson wasted little time in cautiously manoeuvring his way through the shoals, instantly losing HMS

Agamemnon, which ran aground even before entering the channel leading to the enemy line. Cursing his luck, Nelson then had the misfortune to witness two other ships, HMS Russell and HMS Bellona also run aground, restricting their involvement in the battle to come. Anxiously, the frustrated Vice Admiral was forced to make hurried changes in the line, as a result of losing those three ships. Once again, Midshipman Pollard became busy sending up various signals in response to Nelson's amended directives. By that time, he'd become extremely proficient in handling the signalling flags, and impressed others around him with the speed in which he did his job.

Other than the unnecessary loss of those three vessels, so far, all appeared to be going well, and an atmosphere of quiet assurance and confidence remained amongst the British fleet, as they drew closer to the enemy line. That was until, as the attacking ships were almost upon the Danes, Midshipman Pollard was standing on the quarter deck of the Elephant. Suddenly, a shot whistled just a few feet from his head, forcing him to leap to the ground. Finally, the Danish shore batteries had started firing, as soon as the British came into firing range.

Cannons returned fire and very quickly the whole of Nelson's squadron was covered in billowing black smoke, as the guns continued to pound the shore batteries. Following the Vice Admiral's plan, the Danish ships were engaged, with broadsides ploughing into some of the enemy ships, as the

British contingent remained continuously under attack from the shore. They encountered fierce and heavy resistance, partly from the presence of Danish floating batteries, which had gone unnoticed by Nelson, and at one stage, Midshipman Pollard believed he was witnessing another miserable Santa Cruz drama unfolding.

Because of the smoke coming from both the British and Danish guns, Admiral Parker could see little of the battle from his supporting position. What the Commander in Chief did observe were the three grounded ships, two of which were flying signals of distress. There was good reason to believe Nelson's Armada had fought to a standstill, so ordered his flag captain to signal the Vice Admiral to retreat, believing if Nelson was in a position to fight on, he would ignore the order. If he was in a hopeless position, then he could retreat with honour, having been ordered to do so. It was a charitable gesture that was ignored.

"Signal to retreat from flag sir," Midshipman Pollard loudly confirmed, conveying Parker's signal to Nelson, with the background noise of booming broadsides being constantly fired.

The Vice Admiral, who was standing on the quarterdeck of Elephant, viewing the confrontations taking place through a telescope, answered without averting his eye, "Mr. Pollard, you haven't seen that signal, neither have I with my only good eye engaged at looking through this telescope."

"Aye, aye sir."

Nelson was aware, at that time, the guns of the southernmost Danish ships were beginning to fall silent from damage they had sustained, and the ongoing battle was slowly moving northwards and in favour of the British.

"Signal to the bomb vessels to move into position if you please Mr. Pollard."

"Aye, aye sir, bomb vessels to move into position."

As the British ships continued their bombardment, some of the defenders began to successfully withdraw, whilst other Danish ships struck their colours. Some resistance continued, resulting in Nelson sending a note to Crown Prince Frederik, who had been observing the battle from the ramparts of the Citadel in Copenhagen. The Vice Admiral wrote:

'To the brothers of Englishmen, the Danes. Lord Nelson has directions to spare Denmark when she is no longer resisting, but if firing is continued on the part of Denmark, Lord Nelson will be obliged to set on fire the floating batteries he has taken, without having the power of saving the brave Danes who have defended them'.

The offer was sent under a flag of truce, with a Danish-speaking officer, Captain Sir Frederick Thesiger. As a result, all action ceased and Nelson claimed yet another victory. Although no British ships had been lost, many suffered severe damage, as was the case with the Danes. Danish losses totalled over two thousand men killed, wounded or captured. According to Nelson, less than half that number, nine hundred and sixty-three British sailors and officers were killed or wounded.

Nelson was eventually able to secure an indefinite armistice on the understanding that the British would protect Denmark from Russian reprisals, upon leaving the so-called League. Ironically, there was no real need, as news of Tsar Paul having been assassinated soon became known, bringing an end to the League of Armed Neutrality and freeing the Danes from the fear of the Russian guns.

Admiral Parker was recalled to London and ordered to hand over his command to Nelson. Being as the Armed Neutrality League was by then about to end, the new commander of the Baltic fleet, withdrew. He was later created Viscount Nelson of the Nile.

During all the pomp and congratulations that followed, Pollard remarked to his friend and colleague, Midshipman Smiley, that he wondered why the battle had been fought in the first place. With the assassination of the Russian Tsar, the League would have been dismantled in any case. And yet, as with other hostile opponents of Nelson, the Danes had showed they had been no match for the strategic genius of Britain's favourite son.

However, whilst remaining in the Baltic, disturbing news reached the fleet's commander-in-chief. Napoleon was building a bigger fleet of warships than he had possession of prior to his defeat outside Alexandria. It would appear that shortly, yet another threat to the security of Britain would be handed to Nelson to deal with.

Chapter Twelve

Although the British government was aware of the increase in production of war ships by Napoleon, they had signed the Treaty of Amiens, following the French suing for peace. With his army trapped in Egypt and his navy all but destroyed, there was little doubt the usurper to the French throne was in desperate need of time to regroup, and replenish what had been lost during the Battle of the Nile. The temporary end to hostilities between the two countries suited Napoleon, more than it did his opponents. Nelson once again returned to London following the Battle of Copenhagen, greeted by what was becoming a regular event, with crowds of celebrating well-wishers giving the Vice Admiral another hero's welcome.

Having last departed from Portsmouth in his flag ship HMS St George, the country's hero returned in HMS Elephant. On the voyage home, a great deal of attention was given to Nelson, who was suffering from heat stroke and excessive vomiting. As the Vice Admiral fell deeper into a pit of depression, he was convinced his own death was imminent. As the flagship sailed through the choppy waters of the North Sea, it was necessary to assure the crew that Nelson's condition was not life threatening. By the time they reached England, the hero of the hour was fully recovered and back to his normal self.

It was as though, prior to and throughout each battle, Nelson's intensive concentration on beating the enemy totally drained him of all physical resistance. Ironically, all the stress and tension of confrontation and eventual victory, appeared to result in a dramatic reduction of personal resilience, leaving the Vice Admiral exposed to ill health, which seemed to follow each encounter. It was as if the man's vexation went well beyond reasonable human endurance, his constitution incapable of dealing with any ailment, no matter how minor.

At the beginning of Nelson's naval career, Captain Maurice Suckling had been a Royal Navy commander and later a politician sitting in the House of Commons. The gentleman was also an uncle of Horatio Nelson, and had an influence over his nephew's ambition to follow in Suckling's footsteps. After serving with a number of leading naval commanders, the future Vice Admiral rose rapidly through the ranks, until achieving his own command at the young age of twenty.

During a period of serving in the American War of Independence, Nelson earned a reputation for possessing great personal valour and an in-depth knowledge of tactics, which were further enhanced during the Napoleonic wars. Unfortunately, throughout his career he suffered from spates of illness, including sea sickness during his early years, and before being regarded with nationwide heroic recognition. But now, following his recent victories, Nelson was to enjoy the most effective tonic to lift his spirits; the spectacle of flag waving, cheering crowds, as HMS Elephant anchored at Portsmouth.

Arthur Smiley had accepted John Pollard's invitation to stay with him in Plymouth during the forthcoming cessation and fragile peace with France. Both young officers remained unemployed on half pay, until called upon once again to serve their King and country. It was good to be back in a warmer climate, and as they made their way along the coast in a carriage, Smiley remarked to his friend, "I cannot imagine fighting against an enemy at sea without His Lordship being there. I pray to God that Nelson survives the peace."

"How would he not survive?"

"I'm just concerned about his health; you saw how ashen his face was during the voyage back from the Baltic, and although he seems to thrive on warfare, he does appear to have some difficulty with his inner self, when not under the guns of enemy ships."

"Even Vice Admirals can suffer from sea sickness Smiley, and His Lordship will have plenty of time to recover, now we are finally at peace with France."

"But that's what bothers me Pollard. Nelson is the kind of individual who needs to be at war, to survive. I know how deranged that sounds, but I suspect his health will deteriorate and he will be as miserable as sin, during the peace. For how long do you think this peace will last my friend?"

"I thought we had signed a treaty with France."

"I don't think that would mean a great deal to old Boney. I will give it twelve months before we're back at war with the frogs, yet again."

Pollard enquired how long each of them would last on half pay, and Smiley suggested they should cross that bridge when they came to it.

"When we both run out of coin, we can always live on the streets begging."

They both laughed at such an idea, and yet Pollard had a sneaky feeling it might just come to that, if the peace became prolonged. The dismal thought of so many war ships lying idle and unmanned was disturbing, especially as no one really believed the present end to hostilities would last more than a few months, if not weeks.

Mrs. Smolten was the landlady of a renting house overlooking Plymouth harbour where the two former midshipmen sought lodgings. She was a rounded, flushed faced, hearty woman who afforded them a room each with Pollard residing on the top floor, and Smiley in the attic. The rooms were fairly basic, but more than adequate for their needs, especially having spent the last few years sleeping in hammocks in congested areas below decks. The landlady was also sympathetic, knowing her two latest lodgers would be on half pay, and often allowed them time to pay any arrears in their rent.

Shortly after settling into their new digs, Pollard was anxious they should visit his sister, Rose, at the nearby Dog and Doublet Inn, where the young lady had intended on staying following their father's death.

"Have you any relatives you're aware of Smiley?" the youngest of the two naval officers enquired, as they made their way up a steep, cobbled lane. It had begun to rain and both men were walking at a fast pace with their heads bowed down against the inclement weather, being driven by a westerly wind.

"No, I don't believe I have Pollard. I envy the fact you have at least a sister you can call upon."

From the look of disillusionment on his friend's face, Pollard wished he'd never asked the question. He instantly attempted to rectify his friend's discomfort by suggesting that he and Rose would be Smiley's family from thereon.

Both young men were greeted by Mrs. Simpson, the landlord's wife, after being introduced to Arthur Smiley and making comment about how her old friend's son had grown and filled out. She had helped by attending to John Pollard's mother when giving birth to Rose, and had been one of the mourners at Thomas Pollard's funeral.

Having brought drinks across to their table, she left to fetch Rose who was apparently in her room on the first floor of the inn. When John's sister appeared, they both embraced, and her brother remarked how well she looked.

"I can say the same about you John," she answered with a radiant smile, "I've read all about the treaty signed with France and suppose now, you will be out of work."

"Not for long though ma'am," Smiley suggested, "I can't see Napoleon behaving himself for too long."

"Oh, I do hope you are wrong Mr. Smiley." She turned back to her brother and enquired about where he was staying since his return to Plymouth.

"So, what have you been doing with yourself Rose?"

"I'm learning the art of dress making, and helping Mrs. Bright who keeps a shop here in the town centre. It's not much John, but what she can afford to give me helps to pay my way with Mrs. Simpson."

Her brother was pleased the young lady had managed to find some sort of calling and told her so, after kissing his sister on both cheeks.

They sat for an hour or so, catching up on each other's news, until Rose suggested her brother show his friend the harbour.

Pollard smiled at his sister, knowing that both he and Smiley had seen enough of sailing boats in recent months to last them a lifetime, but nevertheless, decided to follow Rose's advice. The walk down to the harbour and back would do both young gentlemen good, and it would give Rose's brother the opportunity to show his friend the rest of Plymouth.

"Are you coming back here for dinner later John?" she asked, "I know Mrs. Simpson won't mind."

"In that case Rose, we shall accept your invitation gladly."

When the two former naval officers reached the lane, which led down to the harbour, Pollard suddenly stopped and stared across at what appeared to be a homeless vagrant, asleep on a wooden bench. He was lying with his back to the two gentlemen, but there was something about his hair and figure, which sparked Pollard's curiosity.

"Bear with me Smiley, I think I know that individual over there," he explained, before stepping across to the sleeping tramp.

He prodded the vagrant, calling out his name.

"Jimmy McNicholas, what on earth..."

The disturbed man, who was obviously in need, surprised Pollard by awaking with a start, and flaying his clenched fists in the air, as if in self-defence of an unexpected violent attack.

The former midshipman stepped back, shocked by the appearance of his old friend. McNicholas was barely identifiable, dressed in rags with a full unkempt beard covering the lower part of his face. What Pollard could see of his face, the down and out looked gaunt and jaundiced.

"Jimmy, it's me, John Pollard."

McNicholas had been a close friend of the unemployed naval officer during their childhood, and in similar fashion to Pollard, had yearned to go to sea. As children they had shared various tales of adventures, and dreams of victorious battles and treasure hunting expeditions. Only, after seeing Pollard leave to fulfil his childhood dreams, McNicholas had remained in Plymouth.

In response to hearing his name being called, the unfortunate individual looked as surprised as John Pollard. His watery eyes stared for a brief moment and then he nodded with a shameful expression on his face, quickly sitting upright on the bench. What in God's name had reduced this man to the pathetic creature now facing Pollard. Both he and Smiley were about to find out.

All three men sat on the same bench, and after introducing Arthur Smiley, both former midshipmen listened intently to the other man's story, grimacing at the odour resulting from a lack of personal hygiene.

James McNicholas explained, after Pollard had left home to enlist, he had got into trouble with the local constable, having been found breaking into a manor house in the countryside surrounding the town. As a result, he was sentenced as a first offender to five years hard labour, having been released from prison just two months previously.

"So here I am, as you find me," he concluded, speaking in a course voice, "Homeless and without a penny to my name. If it wasn't for the soup kitchen down on the front, I'd also be dead by now."

"Life seems to have treated you harshly Jim. I can feel nothing but sympathy for you."

"Don't my old friend, it was my own fault and I swore I would never get caught again." He chuckled, confirming he still had a sense of humour, no matter how vague.

"But what of you? I met your sister a couple of weeks ago and she told me you were serving with Admiral Nelson."

"Yes, we were both serving midshipmen on Nelson's flagship."

Pollard then explained brief details of his and Smiley's experiences at sea, during which time, McNicholas sat listening in wonderment.

"My word John, you have certainly lived a different life to mine, and how an exciting life it must have been, taking part in the Battle of the Nile and more recently the Battle of Copenhagen. The newspapers have reported on very little except the exploits of Nelson. I manage to get hold of a couple of copies every week and use them to help keep me warm at night."

The terrible dilemma in which McNicholas now found himself, shook Pollard, and he couldn't avoid showing his utter dismay. "I take it you haven't been able to find employment?" he asked, stating the obvious.

"Fear not John, nobody wants to employ an ex-jailbird, you can rest assured of that. Are you two still in the navy then, even during the peace?"

"No, we have been paid off and cannot return unless the Admiralty allocate a ship for us."

"And that could be forever, I suppose."

Pollard nodded and confirmed, "As long as the peace holds."

"Then you need to find a money earner in the meantime?"

"We do at that, but nothing illegal Jimmy, we are not..."

"I wasn't going to suggest anything like that John, but I do have an idea where perhaps the three of us could make some coin."

Both former midshipmen glanced dubiously at each other, which didn't go unnoticed by James McNicholas.

"Look, and just hear me out," he begged, "How many men were present at both the Battle of the Nile and Copenhagen?"

"What's on your mind Mr. McNicholas?" Smiley asked, wondering whether the man was about to suggest they forcibly break into the Tower of London and steal the crown jewels.

"At this moment in time, is it not true that the public are thirsting for anything connected with the greatest hero of all time? Both of you gentlemen are also heroes, having been with Nelson during those escapades. I could arrange for you to tell your stories to various gatherings of people who would pay good money to hear them."

McNicholas hadn't changed much. As a mere child, Pollard recalled, he was always coming up with some wild scheme or another. The suggestion he was now putting forward was quite innovative, and both Pollard and Smiley sat in silence, thinking over what John Pollard's friend was suggesting. Would they possibly court trouble by disclosing eye witness accounts of Nelson's most famous victories at sea. Neither could think of any reason why they would. There would certainly be an intensive interest in listening to a pair of the Vice Admiral's officers relate their stories about having served with the great man in victorious battles.

"What kind of gatherings were you thinking about, Jimmy?" Pollard enquired, confirming his interest in the suggestion.

"Where ever people of wealth can be found. At meetings, social functions and attendances such as that. I couldn't go around inviting managers of meeting houses and the like, as soon as they clapped eyes on me, they'd slam the door in my face, but I could select a few appropriate places for you, and once I'm back on my feet, perhaps become your manager for a percentage of the coin you rake in."

It was certainly without risk, and if it helped to swell their coffers, at the same time helping out an old friend, who most certainly was in need of some kind of assistance, there seemed to be no apparent reason why they shouldn't make the attempt.

Pollard turned to Smiley, and asked, "Why not?"

"I think it's a brilliant idea, we can but try. If it doesn't work out well, then what have we to lose?"

"Nothing," McNicholas agreed, "Absolutely nothing, but trust me gentlemen, once people hear about you, then the money should come pouring in."

"Jimmy, you've got yourself a deal," Pollard offered, "What if we pay you twenty percent of what we earn? Would that suffice?"

McNicholas smiled and answered, "That's twenty percent more than I'm getting at present."

The three of them shook hands, cementing their business association, until of course, they received calls from the Admiralty to re-join a ship of war, which was unlikely to be in the near future. It also meant, if successful, they wouldn't have to eventually live on the streets with James McNicholas, begging to survive.

Before they left him, Pollard handed sufficient funds for his friend to get a hot meal and drink, and amazingly, the man began to weep having been afforded such charity. It was obvious that McNicholas hadn't been shown the same charitable benefit for a long time.

Chapter Thirteen

During the lull in fighting between Britain and France, numerous naval lieutenants and various captains became unemployed, being forced to continue living their lives on half pay. During that same period, there were no prizes to be captured and sold on by the Admiralty, distributing more wealth amongst officers and crews, from Admirals to cabin boys. The press gangs disappeared from the streets, and without being at war, the need to man the ships of the line in particular, decreased dramatically. The problem facing many former officers was a virtually impossible task to find berths during a period of peacetime. Some were fortunate, having sufficient funds to survive, but others less contented, finding life more than a little difficult and having to tighten their belts considerably.

Nelson was no exception to his fellow officers, and following his temporary retirement to Britain, the Vice Admiral found himself once again in poor health. He stayed with Sir William and Lady Hamilton, and despite his various ailments, frequently participated in discussions in the

House of Lords, supporting the government of the day. As was his habit, rest appeared to be a non-entity in his daily life, and his workaholic attitude remained a prevalent feature of his character, choosing to ignore his various disabilities and doctor's advice.

As the months passed by, Britain's naval hero agreed to accompany the Hamilton's on a tour of the United Kingdom, and the idea of Nelson making himself more available outside London, appealed to him. Sir William Hamilton was a British diplomat and had served as British Ambassador to the Kingdom of Naples, where his wife Emma, had first met Horatio Nelson. He was also an antiquarian, archaeologist and Member of Parliament, and unfortunately, like the Vice Admiral, wasn't in the best of health. It was thought the country air would be of some benefit to the Knight of the Realm, as well as to his distinguished associate.

The trio visited and made public appearances in Birmingham, Warwick, Gloucester, Swansea, Monmouth and other towns and villages throughout the Kingdom. Whatever location they visited, they were always warmly and enthusiastically welcomed by the various communities. Although Nelson was the main public attraction, Sir William, a Fellow of the Royal Society, would often present the results of his study of the volcanoes, Vesuvius and Etna. Inevitably though, Nelson often found himself being received as a national hero, becoming the centre of attraction during celebrations and events held in his honour.

During that same period, both Britain's military and naval hierarchies kept one eye across the channel, remaining suspicious of what activities were ongoing. Napoleon obviously regarded the fragile peace as a means to an end, his shipbuilding programme continuing with purpose. His armies were increasing in size by the day, and forces were gathering in readiness to invade Great Britain. When news reached London that the French Emperor had ordered the manufacture of a large number of small boats sufficient to carry his army across the channel, concerns were raised in Westminster. The outbreak of war between France and Britain, yet again, was inevitable.

Eventually, Nelson purchased a country estate in Merton, Surrey, where he lived with the Hamilton's until Sir William's death in 1803. Shortly after that event, the peace finally wavered and war broke out, with Britain's favourite son preparing to return to sea. The officers on half pay were quickly recalled, many celebrating, and others not so keen, having quickly settled down to another life away from the Royal Navy. It mattered not; they would all serve King and country when the call finally came.

In the meantime, John Pollard and Arthur Smiley had become the recipients of substantial earnings, as they toured the country presenting details of their experiences when working under Nelson to paying members of the public. With help from James McNicholas, they appeared at numerous refreshment houses, meeting halls and other similar establishments, where formal dinners took place, and of course, where the wealthy congregated. Their tour was a massive success, way beyond anything they could have anticipated.

McNicholas had also financially benefitted from the presentational tours, and was a changed man, living in various upbeat hostelries and attired with the kind of clothes gentlemen were known to wear. The straggly and unkempt beard had disappeared and the former vagrant looked much more civilised and contented. All three of the close friends had been elevated to a much higher social level, with organisers queueing up to secure their services at various functions. Each of the presentations they performed were always met with loud applause and vociferous congratulations, and their fame began to spread away from the south coast, northwards towards London and beyond to the Midlands.

All was well with their new enterprise, until on one occasion, at an inn in Bermondsey, London, they faced their first and only heckler. It happened whilst Pollard and Smiley were individually telling their stories of glorious battles and confrontations under the leadership of Vice Admiral Nelson. Smiley in particular, had developed an expertise for adding drama to his tales, frequently bringing his audience to their feet in applause. Such was the case, as people stood and applauded the two former midshipmen, when a voice suddenly rang out from amongst those gathered in a packed room at the back of the inn.

"You are nothing more than cutpurses and reprobates," the man sitting near to the front yelled out, "I want my money back and you should be paying us for sitting hear listening to such dribble."

"I can assure you sir, nothing we have spoken about this evening is fiction," John Pollard politely told the heckler.

"Cheats, fraudsters, cutpurses, I want my money back," the man yelled back, persisting in making his allegations.

Both Arthur Smiley and James McNicholas leapt from the portable stage and lifted the man from his seat, before physically escorting him from the room, with most of the audience booing the audacity of the heckler. Once outside, Smiley struck him a number of times in the stomach and face with his one fist, before both men left him lying amongst the horse manure on the cobbles outside.

After they returned to the room where the presentations had been taking place, Arthur Smiley apologised to the audience for the untimely interruption, to which he received further applause from the entire gathering. The presentations continued without further interruption and when the stories had been told, the people left, quite happy they had received value for their money, having listened with fascination, to the kind of stories that could be told to grandchildren in the future. The accounts given also endeared Nelson to the public, even more so.

After receiving their dues from the landlord, all three participants left the inn, rejoicing on how much they had made for one evening's entertainment. As they continued walking down a dark narrow cobbled lane, adjacent to the River Thames, and close to where they were staying during their time in the country's capital, they were suddenly attacked by a group of men who came from nowhere. There were four of them, including the heckler from the earlier presentation, and all armed with cudgels. Before any of the victims of the attack really knew what was happening, they were all clubbed to the ground and left lying on the cobbles, groaning and only half conscious. Their earnings for that night's work had been taken.

It was James McNicholas who vowed to track down the robbers and get their money back.

"We lost one night's money, Jimmy," Pollard confirmed, rubbing the back of his head, "It just means performing at one additional presentation to make up for it, and in future we need to be more cautious."

"We need to get our hands on those jackals and get our money back," McNicholas remarked, obviously determined to carry out his threat. But no more was said about the incident, which left all three with aching heads and sore ribs. There was little time to spare before Pollard and Smiley were due to make their next presentation in a refreshment house in Richmond the following evening.

When they arrived at the venue, there was no sign of James

McNicholas. After a successful evening, which culminated in the usual tumultuous applause and cheers for the lads from HMS Elephant, they were just about to leave the premises when their enigmatic friend finally appeared. McNicholas had blood running from his nose, and the knuckles on both of his hands were badly chaffed. And yet, he looked at the two main attractions of the evening with a broad grin across his face. Taking a pile of coins from the pockets of his coat, he handed them to John Pollard, and declared, "Didn't I tell you I would get our money back, and there's four individuals lying on the embankment, who will think twice next time they feel the temptation to rob honest and hard-working jaspers like ourselves."

Both Pollard and Smiley looked at the man with amazement in their eyes, before all three began to laugh out loud. Obviously, McNicholas was a man of many talents, including an ability to successfully probe into the dark activities of London's criminal underworld.

Following a week spent performing in London, all three returned to Plymouth, rejoicing in their success. When Pollard and Smiley stepped into Mrs. Smolten's lodging house, there was a letter for each of them, received from the Admiralty. The call had come more quickly than either of them had anticipated, and they had both been reinstated as midshipmen, and were to report to HMS Victory at Portsmouth.

On the following day, they said their farewells to James McNicholas, who was obviously bitterly disappointed that their money-making venture had finally come to an end. However, the midshipmen's friend and associate, was never again to return to the streets, to live in poverty. With the money he had made from the presentational escapade, he purchased a wig making business, investing wisely and enjoying even more financial success.

Rose travelled with her brother and Arthur Smiley to Portsmouth, where she shared with them, their first sighting of the impressive 104-gun ship of the line, HMS Victory.

"She looks magnificent John," Rose remarked, as the three of them stood on the quayside, looking across at Nelson's most recent flagship.

"So she does Rose, but as silly as it may seem, she is the same ship I was serving on in my dream all those years ago."

"Well, my brother, I'm sure the outcome won't be the same in reality."

Pollard hoped not, but wasn't so sure.

She left them to board their new home, and both men waved from the quarter deck, before Rose turned and walked away.

"Your sister is a fine young lady John," Smiley commented.

"Yes, she is Arthur. I shall miss her, as I always do."

Victory remained at anchor in Portsmouth for two more days following Pollard and Smiley's embarkation, and on the third day, with everything spick and span with the decks scrubbed white, the man, the impressive looking warship had been waiting for, finally arrived. Vice Admiral Nelson was afforded a fifteen-gun salute, as his launch approached his new flag ship. His appointed flag captain was yet again, Captain Hardy, who escorted the senior officer to his cabin after having been piped on board.

John Pollard was to be Nelson's Signal Midshipman once again, and Arthur Smiley celebrated his attachment to Captain Hardy. After watching their Vice Admiral disappear beneath the ship's poop deck, the young man from Plymouth enquired, "Do you think either of us will be given a fifteen-gun salute one day, Mr. Smiley?"

"Not likely, although if Nelson returns from this voyage with another victory to his belt, they'll probably give him a twenty-one-gun salute, normally reserved for Heads of State. In fact, they might just as well make him that now and save the time and trouble. I bet if he was on the other side, the Frogs would have a new emperor."

"What news do you have of the location of the French fleet?"

"None, but a little bird told me last night that we destined for blockade duties at Toulon, which doesn't inspire me much, Pollard." In fact, Midshipman Smiley was absolutely correct in his assumption, and on the night following the arrival of the Vice Admiral, HMS Victory sailed, heading south towards the Mediterranean. At least they were heading for a warmer climate, hot sun and blue skies; that was something to look forward to.

It was with some dismay that, upon learning that the French and Spanish fleets had successfully left Toulon, Nelson took to chasing the enemy across the North Atlantic, with the intention of confronting them in battle. With all sails fully set, he led his ships of the line away from the channel, cancelling his voyage to the Mediterranean. As Victory progressed, the Atlantic rollers greeted her with a vengeance, tossing the vessels about like rocking horses in the water. But the ships managed to remain in sight of each other and progressed north-west at a fair distance from the enemy squadron.

On the second day out in the Atlantic, the sky darkened and a northerly wind teased the seas surface, causing the bow of the Victory to leap up and down like a dolphin dancing across the waves. Nelson retired to his cabin, seasick, and only Captain Hardy and his lieutenants could be seen on the poop deck, watching as a gale approached the British ships.

"Signal, flag to the fleet, keep in close formation," the tall skipper instructed.

"Aye, aye sir, keep in close formation," Pollard repeated, before sending up the appropriate signal.

When the gale hit them, it was with some force. The sky blackened even more and the velocity of the wind increased, bringing with it, a great deal of peril to those crewmen up high, working in the rigging. The waves came at them tall and menacing, crashing over the flag ship's decks. One crewman was swept overboard but was fortunate to be recovered from the water by his shipmates, trembling and scared out of his wits.

For a further two days the weather continued to batter the British squadron like the four horsemen of the apocalypse, determined to sink the human intruders, by taking full advantage of every natural element available. But there were no losses, except for the sanity of a few spinning heads, including that of Vice Admiral Nelson. Eventually a calmness returned and the sun once again showed its face. The sails were filled and the speed of the flotilla increased to re-engage in the pursuit of the French squadron.

On the fifth day out, a call came from the lookout perched high on the main mast.

"To the deck, ship ho sir on the starboard bow."

"Bearing Mr. Caldicote if you please," the First Lieutenant shouted back.

"North by North West sir."

The sail could not yet be seen from the deck, and Midshipman Smiley was sent aloft with a telescope to try and identify the vessel on the horizon.

After scrutinising the shape of the sails, Smiley called to the deck, confirming it was a Frenchie.

"Looks like a French frigate sir," he called back down to the captain, "And she's seen us. She's changed course to avoid us sir."

Hardy immediately instructed the helm to change course and head directly for the enemy ship. He then left the deck and called on the Vice Admiral, who was found sitting in his cabin, looking green faced and obviously still suffering from the movements of the ship. He informed Nelson of the latest development and was asked if any other vessels had been seen.

"No sir, it appears she is alone. If I might suggest, the frigate might be at the tail end of the group we are in pursuit of."

"Or she might have got caught up in that gale, leaving her isolated from the rest of the fleet. I'll come on deck Mr. Hardy." It was a difficult decision for the Commander-in-Chief to make, but Nelson would never have forgiven himself if something drastic would have happened, whilst he was languishing down in his cabin, nursing his sickness in self-pity.

"Aye, aye sir."

The sight of seeing Nelson return to the poop deck at the stern of the flagship was a tonic for the crew, and most of the men watched as their leader viewed the other French frigate through a telescope, now in sight from Victory's decks.

Midshipman Pollard waited anxiously, presuming the Vice Admiral would soon be requiring messages to be sent to the other British ships. He was correct, and Nelson turned to him and instructed, "Signal, flag to fleet, pursue enemy vessel North by North West."

Each of the ships acknowledged and the chase began to run down the targeted enemy vessel, for which there would be no escape from the jaws of the pursuing British warships. It was similar to a pack of terriers chasing a prey through a heavily wooded forest, and there was only ever going to be one winner.

Chapter Fourteen

The British ships quickly closed in on their prey, leaving it desperately outnumbered with nowhere to escape. The speed at which the enemy ship was captured resulted in no real engagement. The French frigate, La Victoire, fired only one broadside as the British ships closed down on her, before striking her colours, realising it was a matter of surrender or be destroyed. Her crew laid down their arms and Nelson himself led the boarding party, impressed by the vessel's name. The French captain gave his parole, after being instructed his ship would be taken back to England as a prize, but refused to answer any questions put to him regarding the current location of the French and Spanish combined fleet somewhere in the vast Atlantic Ocean.

The defeated crew were secured in the hold together with their captain and officers, and Midshipman Pollard was instructed to accompany Nelson and Hardy to the French captain's cabin. Although the maps and charts they discovered were written in French, a continuous line drawn across one chart revealed the information they were seeking.

"Why the Caribbean?" asked the English captain, having to crouch down to avoid hitting his head on the overhead beams inside the small room.

"The West Indies Hardy," Nelson answered, "But the purpose of the voyage is for us to discover. At least, by God's will, we now know where our enemy is heading." Nelson then turned to his midshipman and instructed him to signal the fleet for all captains to attend the flag ship, as soon as they returned to Victory. The Vice Admiral also took possession of the frigate's logs and other documents that would be worthy of further scrutiny.

La Victoire hadn't been fired upon and was in perfect condition for refitting and becoming a part of the British fleet. A small crew was left under the supervision of a lieutenant, to take her back to Portsmouth, whilst the remainder of the British ships continued across the North Atlantic, heading for the West Indies and a confrontational battle with the combined French and Spanish. However, one further unwelcome episode crossed their path before reaching the Caribbean.

Unexpectedly and without warning a lull in the weather enveloped the British convoy, leaving the sea perfectly calm, and without the slightest breeze. Each of the ships was like a motionless statue, or model posing for an artist's canvas. The sails were reefed and there was no movement, delaying further progress. It was indeed, strangely surreal, seeing Nelson's ships all standing hove to, as if at anchor, but nothing could be done until the winds picked up again. It was frustrating and yet another enforced delay taunted the British.

"We could always wet the sails sir, to provoke movement," Captain Hardy suggested, but Nelson refuted the idea, telling his friend and flag captain, time would be better served studying the maps and charts taken from La Victoire. And that is exactly what both Nelson and Hardy did, during the few days of inactivity.

One docket seized from La Victoire contained maps of the English Channel and Atlantic Ocean, with lines of vessels close to the French shore. What both the Vice Admiral and his flag captain quickly realised was that they had inadvertently come across Napoleon's plans to invade Britain. The various locations of the British channel fleet were also marked across another map, but there was no indication of any date when the invasion was to take place.

As the days passed by, with the fleet helplessly floating on the surface of the Atlantic, unable to fill their sails, it soon became obvious the crew on Victory were becoming disenchanted. No matter how many drills and rehearsals they were subjected to, widespread apathy soon began to surface.

Midshipman Pollard made a suggestion to the First Lieutenant that they held a race between two selected halves of the crew. The race would comprise of two teams climbing up the rigging of all three masts and back down again, beginning with the foremast near to the bow, the main mast in the centre of the quarter deck, and the mizzen mast at the stern. The winning team would be given an extra rationing of rum, if the captain agreed, and the losers would have to entertain the rest of the ship's company on the night following the race.

Captain Hardy gave the idea his blessing, and suggested, if successful, the other ships might well consider repeating the process. The appropriate arrangements were made. The crew of over eight hundred men were divided into two teams, blue and red, and each team was invited to select the fittest twenty amongst them to compete. The idea was a master stroke and very quickly, there was a buzz that went all around the vessel, with the men arguing about which team would be the likely winners.

Even Nelson appeared on the poop deck to watch proceedings, as the first two seamen waited to begin the race. Being as the idea had come from Midshipman Pollard, he was given the honour of starting the race, and stood on the quarter deck holding a whistle in one hand. The Vice Admiral nodded and the whistle was blown. Both starters leapt up the rigging of the foremast like two monkeys, against a background of cheers and encouragement from both team's members.

Up they scaled, touching the top gallant mast, before dropping back down to the deck, running to the main mast and repeating the operation. By the time they reached the mizzen mast, the blue team member was marginally in front, and as soon as his feet dropped back down to the deck, the next team member took off from the bow of the ship.

Pollard was amazed at the speed in which the competitors tackled the rigging, leaping up the netting without missing a foothold. The entire ship became a cauldron of excitement as the race progressed, and it was touch and go, which team would finish first. Finally, the red team, having overtaken their opponents won the competition. Whilst the blue team booed the winners, the triumphant crewmen were allocated the extra portion of rum promised.

In his wisdom, Captain Hardy also granted half extra ration to the losers, for having participated, but insisted the blue team would put on some entertainment that same evening. And so it was, with the deck lights turned up, the blues orchestrated a performance that would be long remembered. Much to the amazement of those watching, there were jugglers and trapeze artists displaying their individual talents. One older crew member sang a sea shanty, which brought tears to most of the audience's eyes, and then came the comedians, the pranksters and imitators, one soul actually pretending to be Lord Nelson himself, whose antics brought a smile to the Vice Admiral's face. The whole affair had been a huge success and Midshipman Pollard was thanked by many for his innovation.

It was following that evening's performance, Nelson called Hardy to his cabin. Having studied the charts taken from La Victoire, he indicated the line drawn across the Atlantic, stopping just short of the West Indies, and another broken line visible and appearing to reveal the route back to the Mediterranean. But there was no indication of any part of the West Indies that was intended to be visited.

"What do you make of that Hardy?" the Vice Admiral enquired.

The flag captain stood bowed over that one singular chart, staring down at the two lines drawn across the ocean, but not going anywhere in particular and without any evident purpose.

Finally, he answered the question posed with his opinion. "A ruse sir. There can be no other logical reason; a ruse to draw us away from Toulon, depleting the blockade fleet, before returning."

"Yes, and I suspect we have fallen for it. How many ships did they tell us had left Toulon?"

"The number twenty was mentioned my Lord, the majority being ships of the line."

"Leaving the remainder of the French and Spanish to come out of hiding and attack what was left of our Mediterranean blockade."

"And allow supply ships through to deliver to the French, some of their basic necessities."

Nelson stared up at Hardy and shook his head. He then suggested, "We have been chasing ghosts captain and should be hanged from the yardarm for having been so stupidly gullible."

"An extremely devious plan, which if I am not mistaken, would have been devised by the French. Perhaps by Napoleon himself."

"Turn her around Mr. Hardy as soon as the wind gets up. We're heading back."

"Aye, aye sir."

Unfortunately, the lull which had stranded the British fleet continued for another two days. Under no circumstances could either Hardy or Nelson inform the crew of their suspicions, not even the other officers, and especially as the fleet was immobile so far away from where there was every possibility the French and Spanish were causing havoc with the blockade in the Mediterranean. Nelson imagined supply ships queueing up to enter the French ports with vital supplies to support their war effort. To say he was annoyed at himself for having been cajoled in such a way, was an under-statement, and he remained in his cabin until the acknowledgement he had been waiting for was eventually heard.

"South Westerly sir." It came from the main mast look out, and every officer on board, including Nelson arrived on the decks. The sails were unfurled and filled with a breeze that was skimming off the sea's surface. It wasn't exactly of gale proportions, but was sufficient to allow the ships to make way.

"Signal South by South East Mister Pollard, and then flag to all captains, to the flag ship, if you please."

"Aye, aye sir, South by South East and all captains to the flagship," the midshipman answered, before realising the co-ordinates given by Nelson, were for the fleet to return in the opposite direction, away from the Caribbean. They were heading back to the Mediterranean without having sighted the enemy fleet.

"All ships acknowledged sir."

"Yes, thank you."

"I reckon it's a trick the old man has devised to trap the Dons and Frogs," Midshipman Smiley remarked quietly.

"In what way?" asked Pollard.

"If I knew that, I'd be the Admiral. But I wouldn't mind betting he's got something up his sleeve. I reckon in a short time, everybody will be signalled to slow down, to give the enemy time to catch up with us."

For once, Smiley was wrong. There was no slowing down, and the British fleet with all sails set, progressed quickly and in earnest to catch up with the time wasted during the lull. The word passed down by Nelson was that the enemy was no longer in the West Indies and was returning on a different tack. All hands were needed to perform at their best in getting the fleet back to the Spanish coast as quickly as possible.

Just as the lull in the weather had caught the British out so unexpectedly, the wind surprisingly got up and was backing a little southerly, which the fleet took advantage of under full sail. Men were constantly reefing and unfurling, changing tack and hauling in, all in an effort to increase speed, with the Signal Midshipman having to constantly instruct the fleet to remain in close formation. There was no time to wait for stragglers, and the Vice Admiral by then, had informed the other captains of what he suspected, that the blockade at Toulon had been weakened by a French and Spanish ruse. Even when other vessels outside the fleet were sighted, they were not investigated or approached. Nelson was like a cat on a hot tin roof, frequently appearing on deck and looking towards the bow, as if expecting to see the Spanish coast suddenly appear, but of course to no avail.

By the time HMS Victory reached a position just off the Spanish coast, a call was received from the main mast lookout that a sail had been sighted.

"North to North West sir," the lookout confirmed.

Nelson was called, and on this occasion, didn't refuse to ignore the warning. Instead he ordered two of his frigates to intercept and report back as quickly as possible. What was taken possession of, was a commercial vessel, making its way into Cadiz with supplies of cotton and timber. A prize crew was quickly designated to take the cutter northwards to Portsmouth and the fleet continued around the Spanish coast, entering the

Mediterranean with Nelson impatient to make contact with the blockade outside Toulon.

When they finally arrived, it was with great relief the Vice Admiral learned that the blockade had been reinforced by ships from the channel fleet. Now with Nelson's additional eight ships of the line and three frigates, the blockade of Toulon was strengthened further. However, during the months that followed, Nelson's health didn't improve and his seasickness persisted, so much so, Midshipman Smiley again remarked to his friend that the Admiral was not looking in the best of health.

"I hope he will be fit enough to command when we finally face the Frogs," he whispered, after ensuring no one was within earshot.

"Of course he will," Pollard commented, "The problem the Admiral is having, is this unceasing bad weather." The young man from Plymouth was referring to the daily squalls and storms, which had been plaguing the ships of the blockade in recent weeks. He was correct that in such inclement weather, it would be a nightmare for anyone suffering from seasickness. But that wasn't Nelson's principle problem. He was in earnest need of more intelligence regarding the enemy's strength, and as a result, sent two of his frigates, the 38-gun Active, and the 32-gun Amphion to assess the French moored inside Toulon harbour. When they returned, the news they carried was that the enemy ships totalled the same number as the British.

Nelson was aware that those ships responsible for drawing him away from the Mediterranean, would soon return, giving the French and Spanish a distinct advantage. And yet, the shallow waters in the approach to Toulon harbour made it too risky to take the squadron in to attack the enemy whilst at anchor. For the time being, he felt like an insect trapped inside a spider's web.

The squalls and rain were replaced in typical Mediterranean fashion with a cloudless sky and a hot sun, which beat down relentlessly on the decks, creating a different kind of discomfort to the crews of the blockade ships. No one was spared from the immense heat. Those working on the upper decks were stripped from their waists upwards, exposing sweat covered ribcages, and those trying to rest below decks had to suffer unusually warm and clammy conditions. The heat wave continued for two weeks, during which time the water supplies had to be rationed, before being replenished by vessels out of Gibraltar.

What little breeze there was, disappeared one particularly dark night, which found the two midshipmen standing at the stern rail looking across towards the Spanish coastline.

"There's a storm brewing," the one-armed Arthur Smiley remarked, "And I reckon it will be upon us by morning."

Pollard agreed with his friend, and suggested they should get some sleep before the thunder and lightning reached them, with all the havoc a storm at sea usually produced.

At daybreak, black clouds could be seen coming towards the fleet from the east and Captain Hardy instructed Clyde Napier, the First Lieutenant, who had served under Nelson on the St George, to reef the sails and set the royals, in readiness for what was about challenge the fleet. Then it came: firstly, the thunder rolled and both Pollard and Smiley watched as forks of lightning could be seen in the distance appearing to be poured from a jug into the ocean on the horizon. Then the sky went as black as pitch and the winds blew in hurricane fashion, changing the sea into awesome white flagged rollers, striking each side of Victory. She rolled and dipped as if out of control, like some trapped victim, with the water crashing over the upper decks.

Hardy was shouting orders from near the mizzen mast, as the area around the Victory suddenly lit up with sheet lightening flashing across the ill-tempered sky.

"This won't last long," Smiley suggested, "Mark my words, a storm as ferocious as this will soon blow over."

Pollard didn't answer, busy watching a seaman grasping hold of the rigging, at the front of the ship, as Victory's bow dipped beneath the waves. One crashed over the fore deck, completely covering the same mariner, who stood his ground, but looked a little shaken by the experience.

Smiley was soon proved to be right in his assumption and as quickly as the fierce wind had appeared, it disappeared, leaving the sea calmer, yet still accompanied by the thunder and lightning. It was strange the way quietness prevailed, and the older of the two midshipmen was quick to confirm, "What did I tell you, Pollard."

Captain Hardy, who was standing nearby on the poop deck, turned and advised the crew that there was more to come, and the final performance would be much more devastating than they had experienced so far. His judgement was based on vast experience of Mediterranean freak storms, and he was quickly proved to be right.

Suddenly, and without warning, the winds returned with a vengeance, and both Hardy and Napier continued bawling out various orders to the crew, as the sea picked up again and the crashing waves began to unsettle the ship once more. One colossal wave hit the Victory on the portside, almost turning her completely over. She remained on her side for what seemed like an eternity as the threatening waves continued to pour over one side of her exposed copper bottom. Pollard was convinced she was about to sink, and wasn't the only one trying to come to terms with such fear. Then, slowly she corrected herself and returned to an upright position, again with her captain screaming out orders for the crew to keep her as steady as possible. There was no doubt, the ship had been kept afloat by a slight break in the storm and the incredible seamanship of both Hardy and Napier.

Finally, the last of the storm moved away and Nelson made his first appearance on deck, looking pale faced and at death's door. He had remained in his cabin throughout, obviously engaged in his own struggle against seasickness.

By that time the sea had calmed, there were streaks of blue in the sky above, with the Mediterranean sun trying hard to break through.

"How did we fare Hardy?" he quietly asked.

"No losses sir, perhaps just a few shaken souls."

The Vice Admiral called for his Signal Midshipman and instructed Pollard to signal, flag to the fleet, report any loss or damage.

Each ship of the line came back with responses similar to that given by Hardy. It took three days before the pumps being worked below deck managed to restore the ship back to her normal self. During the period in which the British fleet had been literally battered by the elements, the forces of the French and Spanish had enjoyed the shelter of Toulon and Cadiz; a fact not overlooked by Nelson.

Chapter Fifteen

Whereby Vice Admiral Nelson's preference would have been to take the battle to the French by attacking their ships, where ever they might be, the Admiralty's decision to contain the enemy by blockading the French and Spanish ports, and prevent commercial ships from delivering necessary supplies, appeared to be working effectively. In addition to the blockade of Toulon, Admiral Cornwallis had fifteen ships patrolling the channel, effectively blockading the French Vice Admiral Joseph Ganteaume's twenty-one ships confined at Brest. Vice Admiral Calder had eight vessels watching over Ferrol, where four French ships of the line were hemmed in, together with eight Spanish war ships. Nine French and Dutch vessels were trapped in the Netherlands by Admiral Keith's eleven ships, and Rear Admiral Graves had five enemy ships restricting the port at Rochefort.

Albeit, Napoleon's land army had achieved success against other European nations, his navy was failing miserably at sea. The Emperor's order for numerous boats to be built in readiness for an intended invasion of England, had been completed, but no advancement could be made until the threat of the Royal Navy had been removed.

Nelson and Hardy had misread the intentions of the French and Spanish, when suspecting the voyage to the West Indies was a ruse to draw a squadron of British ships away from the Mediterranean. In fact, the French Admiral Villeneuve had been instructed by Napoleon to stop the supply of necessities from the Caribbean to Great Britain, a plan which had met with little success, much to Villeneuve's discredit.

Napoleon was desperate for his navy to achieve some success, and from Paris he ordered Admiral Ganteaume to move his fleet from Brest to Ferrol and put Admiral Calder's blockade out of action, releasing the twelve French and Spanish war ships being prevented from setting sail. The Emperor's intention was for them to then move across the Atlantic to join Villeneuve's fleet and return to the channel with what would consist of a total of forty-four ships. Such a flotilla would be sufficient to crush the British resistance and enable Napoleon's army to execute his invasion plan.

However, Napoleon knew very little about conducting a war at sea, and the British blockades, especially that led by Cornwallis at Brest, remained effective and Ganteaume's squadron was kept immobilised. It was a massive hindrance to the French intentions and her invasion army was forced to remain unemployed at Boulogne, much to the satisfaction and relief of the British.

As the months passed by, Nelson was already aware of the danger of scurvy aboard his vessels should his men be deprived of fresh fruit or vegetables. The Vice Admiral had already lost most of his upper teeth to the disease, and did all in his power to prevent it from raising its ugly head amongst the crews of his fleet. The need for fresh supplies of food, including lemons and onions became imperative, so he organised supplies from various ports around the Mediterranean, in particular Roses in Spain, where Nelson's contact there, Mr. Gayer, a wine merchant, managed to frequently supply the Vice Admiral with beef and onions. The same ally also created an effective intelligence network across Spain, providing updated information on the movements of the Dons ships. It appeared from what he learned, only the British and Villeneuve's fleet were actually at sea.

It was also necessary for Nelson to keep up the morale of his officers and crews and was found to excel in this attempt, rotating his ships used for surveillance missions, thus reducing boredom amongst the men. The British commander also spent a great deal of his time with those officers who didn't take part in his frequent meetings with the captains, including the midshipmen, and entertaining them on board the Victory. They were to continue giving him their trust, loyalty and confidence, and it was these leadership skills that set him apart from other high-ranking officers.

Although the health of his men was exceptional in the circumstances in which they worked, the same couldn't be said about Nelson himself. In addition to suffering from constant seasickness, he was always in need of rest and sleep as a result of the strain placed on him by his command. Also, his eyesight suffered greatly from the demands of writing and reading during the times he allowed himself some candle lit solitude in his cabin. Although advised by the ship's surgeon to reduce the time he spent with his personal letter writing, such advice was ignored and Nelson failed to break his habits.

In contrast to the British Commander-in-Chief's methods of dealing with his men's boredom and restlessness, the French troops in Boulogne were never afforded the same consideration, and continued to suffer from the apathy resulting from inactivity. Napoleon was frustrated by the British tactics of blockading his ships, and was angry at the resulting delay. Eventually, he reluctantly withdrew his army from the French coast and directed them to fight Russia and Austria, as an alternative to invading Britain. The intended invasion had been defeated without one single shot having been fired.

It was on one particular Mediterranean morning, when the dawn was breaking over the horizon, a brig was sighted heading towards Victory. A messenger was allowed to board the flagship, but rather than disturb Nelson who was resting in his cabin, Captain Hardy took possession of the sealed envelope sent by Admiral Cornwallis, and personally took it to his

Vice Admiral.

After handing the missive to Nelson, he turned to leave, but was told to remain, whilst the contents of the envelope were read.

"So, it seems the jackal has arrived back in the channel," Nelson confirmed, as if talking to himself, "By jove Hardy, Villeneuve and his squadron have been chased out of British waters and are now trapped in Cadiz by Collingwood."

"That's excellent news sir, but I fear, he will still offer a threat to us."

Nelson looked up at Hardy and nodded in agreement.

"But remember, he's just voyaged to the West Indies and back. I should think his men will be exhausted and his ships in need of repair, those probably being the reasons why he turned and ran, rather than engage Collingwood's ships in battle. This would be an ideal time to take the war to the enemy, of only..."

"So, you are considering a frontal attack on Cadiz?" Hardy enquired.

Nelson sat there for a moment in silence, giving careful consideration to Hardy's suggestion, before confirming, "No, the odds would be too much against us. The only place to guarantee success against the French and Spanish is seaward, where they couldn't keep running into ports and hiding beneath their shore batteries. We need to somehow draw the blighters from out of their hidey-holes."

But Nelson's way of thinking was meaningless, as shortly afterwards, still suffering from anxiety, stress and poor eyesight, he was ordered home by the Admiralty. The temporary break was intended to afford their most treasured possession the opportunity to restore himself to good health. It was a rare occasion when the Vice Admiral accepted the order with some relief, before leaving the Mediterranean on board HMS Victory. The long wait whilst carrying out blockade duties, had taken its toll on the mentality of every sailor and officer involved, and Nelson was no exception.

Of course, it also meant a return to England for Midshipmen Pollard and Smiley and both young officers planned to take full advantage of the privilege. As Nelson's ship headed northward towards the channel, Smiley wondered if they would have sufficient time to look up James McNicholas, and perhaps earn more coin visiting various places and reiterating their public presentations.

"I fear not my friend," John Pollard answered, "It would be folly not to be at the commander's beck and call. I cannot see us being away from the Mediterranean for too long."

"I suppose you are right Pollard, but I wished you weren't always so pessimistic."

"I think we should follow in his Lordship's footsteps, and in what little time we are given, rest up and live an idle life."

"On a midshipman's pay?"

Pollard laughed, and quickly remarked, "Now who's being pessimistic?"

During the short period ashore, Nelson remained at his Merton home, which he regarded as paradise, together with his mistress, Emma Hamilton, and their young daughter, Horatia. His two youngest officers stayed at Mr. and Mrs. Simpson's Inn in the heart of Plymouth. There they undertook lengthy walks conversing joyfully with Rose, who boasted about how well her dress making career was progressing, and eventually managing to bore the pants off both men. They were a long way from the rigours of maintaining a ship at war, but were enjoying the respite.

When their favourite subject of life at sea came to the fore, they were bombarded by a string of questions thrown at them by John Pollard's enthusiastic sister.

"How do you avoid being hit by enemy fire?"

"What's the food like on board Victory?"

"What kind of man is Captain Hardy?" And so forth. But they were happy to indulge the lady, at least until the subject of conversation returned to dress making.

Nelson's assumption that Villeneuve's crews would be exhausted following their Atlantic crossings was an accurate one. Both his ships and men were in poor shape, but the French fleet as a whole still outnumbered the British. If they should ever manage to get past the British blockades, they could seriously damage trade convoys heading for Britain. They could also possibly stop British troops from meeting with the Russians to take back Italy from Napoleon. But above all, the combined enemy fleet would be a major threat to those British ships in the channel. Only Nelson was confident the French and Spanish would not come out of their safe havens in a hurry, confident that Villeneuve would have no overwhelming desire to fight.

The Lords of the Admiralty were becoming more anxious by the day, although it had been their decision to insist on Nelson being given time to recover back at home. The French fleet had to be destroyed sooner rather than later, and after allowing their most popular Admiral sufficient time to convalesce, and save face by recalling him earlier than had first been planned, once again he was sent for. On this occasion, it was made clear to Nelson he would return to the Mediterranean as sole Commander-in-Chief.

Both Pollard and Smiley didn't wait for their orders to be delivered. As soon as they read in the newspapers that Nelson had been recalled to the Mediterranean fleet, again they bid Pollard's sister Rose, farewell, and were off to Portsmouth to re-join Victory. On the journey, Midshipman Pollard read from an article in one newspaper saying, 'No other officer could have the skill, knowledge and genius required to totally annihilate the enemy'.

He looked across at his friend, who slapped a closed fist into the palm of his other hand and declared, "This time Pollard, we are going to kick that fat arse of Bony's once and for all."

"And what of the Spanish? Remember we shall have to take on the Dons as well as the French."

"Bah, once we annihilate the Frogs, the Spanish will capitulate quickly enough. Their ships are in a worst condition than the French."

As far as the two midshipmen were concerned, the urgency behind Nelson's recall meant only one thing; on this occasion there was a strong intention to take the fight to the enemy; a fight which would finally dictate which nation would rule the seas from thereon.

As the two midshipmen were entering the harbour at Portsmouth, Horatio Nelson was kneeling at the side of his sleeping daughter's bedside. He said a prayer for her and his beloved Emma, before leaving Merton, elegantly dressed in his full ceremonial uniform with both his honours and medals being proudly displayed.

During Nelson's return journey to Portsmouth, he felt melancholic, although determined to do whatever duty was demanded of him. He decided to put into writing another prayer, addressed to his daughter, Horatia:

'Friday night at half past ten, drove from dear, dear Merton where I left all which I hold dear in this world, to go to serve my King and country. May the Great God whom I adore enable me to fulfil the expectations of my country and if it is His good pleasure that I should

return, my thanks will never cease being offered up to the Throne of His mercy. If it is His good providence to cut short my days upon Earth, I bow with the greatest submission relying that He will protect those so dear to me that I may leave behind. His will be done. Amen, Amen, Amen.'

The diary entry showed that, although when in a brooding mood, Nelson had always hoped for a glorious death in a victorious battle. In reality, he remained hopeful that would not be the case, and that he would live a long and prosperous life with those he loved so dearly.

The Victory's crew watched as their Commander-in-Chief was rowed out to his flag ship, with Captain Thomas Hardy at his side. A large crowd of people had gathered to bid him farewell, and cheered, applauding as Nelson left the quayside. He turned to his flag captain and said, "I had their hurrahs before. I have their hearts now." The expectation perceived from Nelson's recall to duty was that the war at sea would soon be over, with yet another outstanding victory for Britain's favourite son. The same anticipation was confidently widespread amongst those who served under the Vice Admiral. This next stage in the Napoleonic Wars was to be Britain's High Noon, and the expectation level of the whole country reached epic proportions.

He boarded Victory to the usual sound of pipes reserved only for an Admiral, and before sailing back to the Mediterranean, stopped at

Plymouth, Midshipman Pollard's home town, to collect two other ships of the line, HMS Ajax and HMS Thunderer.

As the vessels sailed southwards once again, there was a general sense of exhilaration, in anticipation of a confrontation with both the French and Spanish fleets. Pollard remained at his post throughout the voyage, close and within earshot of Lord Nelson, awaiting orders to signal other ships. As they passed through the choppy waters of the Bay of Biscay, once again Nelson became isolated in his cabin, suffering from his usual infernal bouts of seasickness.

"I reckon that short break back in England has done nothing for him," Midshipman Smiley remarked, in his usual pessimistic manner.

"You don't know that."

"At eight bells, he came up on deck and looked as green as the rawest recruit at Portsmouth."

"So what, if he suffers from seasickness? While Lord Nelson survives, every member of this crew will follow him. You must know that Smiley."

"I suppose so."

"By the way Pollard, I was considering asking for your sister's hand in marriage. What do you think my friend?"

That suggestion hit John Pollard like an unseen cannon ball suddenly coming out of the fog and striking home. For a moment he just stared across at his friend, speechless, unable to think of any kind of response.

"Well? Would you give me your blessing?"

"Of course, have you mentioned your intentions to Rose?"

"Not yet, but I thought I would converse with you beforehand. Would I have your blessings Pollard?" he repeated.

Smiley's friend placed an arm around his shoulder and reiterated, "Haven't I just said so, provided of course, Rose agrees."

"Of course she will. Why on earth should any young lady reject the advances of such a handsome gentleman, and one who can fight with one arm tied behind his back?"

That caused them both to laugh out loud, and attract the attention of the second lieutenant, who was standing nearby.

"Remember your station gentlemen," was the warning.

Both nodded and bowed their heads, but unable to stop sniggering like a couple of children having just won a doughnut at the fair.

Smiley was wrong in refusing to accept Nelson's break away from the fleet had been beneficial. The Vice Admiral was rejuvenated and more determined than ever to later return to England with another victory in his grasp; perhaps the greatest victory of them all. Three days later, he sent HMS Euryalus to inform Admiral Collingwood, he was ready to take over command of the fleet. With Britain's most prominent and effective naval senior officer now in charge in the Mediterranean, the chances of routing out the French and Spanish had increased ten-fold. The wily strategist was confident of success, except this time, he was determined to completely destroy the French and their allies, the Spanish. It would take nerve and commitment, and Nelson was fully aware he had both of those strengths, but surprise tactics would be his guarantee of success.

Chapter Sixteen

After returning to the Mediterranean as Commander-in-Chief of the fleet, it was necessary to observe any of the activities of the enemy and to quickly report back, should there be any attempt to run the blockade. Nelson's earlier desires to face the French and Spanish head on, had changed somewhat, appreciating the advantage his adversaries would gain from the shore batteries. To attack enemy ships in harbour would be folly, so the Vice Admiral decided to be patient and continue to play the waiting game, keeping his fleet in blockading formation. He did need to strengthen his observations on Toulon though, and quickly dispatched two look-out ships. He then engaged himself in formulating a number of strategic options he considered to be the most effective in defeating the enemy, working alone in his cabin. In fact, he spent a great deal of his time in isolation, planning and scheming with the current size and condition of the enemy at the forefront of his mind.

Shortly after Nelson's arrival off Cadiz, Vice Admiral Cuthbert

Collingwood joined the squadron in HMS Royal Sovereign, a 100-gun ship of the line. The fleet commander wasted little time in enlightening Collingwood of his most favoured plan. He called it the 'Nelson Touch' and, as would be expected of the Commander-in-Chief, the proposed plan flew in the face of conventional strategies for a sea battle. In normal circumstances a fleet would line up parallel to that of the enemy and fire broadsides on one-to-one encounters. That was the kind of strategic plan Nelson's enemy would be anticipating. However, he had other ideas on how to surprise the other side, similar to those deployed at Alexandria, which had proved to be so successful.

He once again relied on the element of surprise, whereby, rather than approaching the enemy in one line, he intended to sail in two separate columns; one led by himself and the other by Collingwood. Each column would then sail straight through the French and Spanish line, gaining the rear and negating the enemy's advantage in having more ships. Such a manoeuvre would render the enemy's front line ineffective, until they could turn around and re-join the battle. Nelson hoped that by then, the tables would have turned sufficiently, and his own fleet would be in a position to outnumber and outgun the enemy, pummelling the remainder of their ships before they could once again face him head on.

It was most certainly an innovative scheme, which gained the approval of Collingwood and the captains. However, they also acknowledged the risks involved. The biggest problem would have to be met by those British ships positioned at the front of the two columns. They would be vulnerable and exposed to enemy broadsides, which meant those ships could take quite a beating before even reaching their opposite numbers. Therefore, Nelson placed what he regarded as his two strongest vessels, Victory and Royal Sovereign at the head of each column. As was pointed out to him on a number of occasions when meeting his captains, he himself, would be at extreme risk from enemy fire. The Commander-in-Chief counteracted that concern by declaring that his presence at the front of the attack would serve to inspire his men, boosting their morale and determination to win the day. He was also aware that those same crewmen would have to show nerves of steel, being unable to inflict any serious damage to the enemy ships, having been ordered to hold return fire until they had broken through the Spanish and French line. It quickly became apparent that both Victory and Royal Sovereign could become sacrificial lambs, with the two leading commanders on board.

Every new battle strategy carried risk with it, and Nelson explained that to the others. However, by surprising the enemy with an all-out melee, success would be achieved by superior and faster, more accurate gunnery. He had no doubt, the high morale of his well-trained, highly disciplined men would carry the day. That was his principle hope to achieve victory.

Also, following the confidence he had displayed with his captains at the

Battle of the Nile, he would do the same here, dismissing the idea of signals and allowing them to choose each of their own targets. Nelson was concerned that by using signals during a melee, they could easily be misread or not even seen at all.

"No captain can do very wrong if he places his ship alongside that of an enemy," he advised.

It was generally accepted that in the ensuing and inevitable chaos, as the enemy line was torn apart, it would be every ship for itself, and that, in Nelson's strategic thinking, was another key to success. By placing his complete faith and confidence in his captains, he would be instilling in them the kind of self-belief that enabled them to attack the enemy without having to await orders from their Commander-in-Chief.

As the fleet off Cadiz strengthened with the arrival of HMS Agamemnon, Nelson's favourite ship from England, and a little later, HMS L'aimable, there was a buzz of anticipated excitement throughout the ships' crews. A total of thirty-three British vessels were now assembled and Nelson ensured they kept well out of sight of the shoreline, not wanting the enemy to see how strong the opposition was.

Both Midshipmen, Pollard and Smiley, watched eagerly, the activity between each of the vessels, including visits from supply ships from Gibraltar. It was obvious a battle was imminent and the general expectation was that when it came, it would finally inflict total devastation on the defeated nation.

"How long must we wait do you think Pollard, before they come out and fight us?"

"I suspect whenever they are ready to, and not when we would prefer them to."

"I cannot see why we just don't go into the ports shielding them and give them hell."

"Have no fear, his Lordship knows what he's doing. I suspect we shall be seeing the enemy soon enough."

Nelson had little doubt the first move made by the enemy would be led by Villeneuve, who was contained inside the harbour of Cadiz. It was important for the French in particular, to be kept under close observation, and to do so, required a chain of communication. He placed several of his frigates close to the harbour mouth, and then positioned HMS Defence and HMS Agamemnon seven to ten leagues west of Cadiz. HMS Mars and HMS Colossus were positioned between the observing frigates and the Victory, which allowed him constant communication. He was determined not to allow the French the opportunity of evading him, as had been the case earlier when Villeneuve had left for the West Indies. To ensure he would be ready to attack any effort to leave the safety of the Cadiz batteries, he formed his fleet into the order of Sailing.

Over the course of a couple of days, Midshipman Pollard was busy signalling the fleet from the flagship.

"He's depending on them trying to run away," Smiley remarked.

"But why would they run my friend?" Pollard enquired, "It's common knowledge, the French and Spanish combined, will outnumber us."

"Think about it, Pollard, some of those French Admirals would have been present when we burnt their tails at Alexandria. Would you want to fight us again after that?"

"You have a point, Mr. Smiley."

In fact, Smiley's assumption was an accurate one. There did exist French Admirals and senior officers who had experienced previous battles against Nelson, and were reluctant to offer resistance on a second occasion.

One other feature existed, which was beyond Nelson's knowledge. Admiral Villeneuve, who was the appointed commander of the combined fleets of the French and Spanish, wasn't having an easy time of things. He had unsuccessfully faced Nelson at Alexandria, and was now aware his old enemy had joined the British fleet in the Mediterranean. The French Admiral knew exactly what the British Commander-in-Chief was capable of and was not confident of success. Villeneuve was also aware from first-hand experience that Nelson had at his disposal, better guns, with less recoil, better gunpowder, and his crews were far quicker and more accurate when performing in battle. Indeed, if he could avoid a confrontation, he would.

One other factor, which Nelson had become aware of, was that the French and Spanish crews didn't get on with each other. It was widely known that even the captains argued when faced with decisions as to what to do. In fairness to Villeneuve, he tried to resolve the problem of incompatibility by mixing the French and Spanish ships of the line, so that glory and blame would be shared equally, reducing the risk of them deserting one another. But, as a result of his failure at the Battle of the Nile, the Spanish Admirals and captains didn't trust him, and thought him to be incapable of leading a major action. Thereby, the morale of the enemy was extremely low, much to Nelson's satisfaction.

As the British fleet waited patiently, like a cat waiting for a mouse to come out of its hole, the pressure increased on Villeneuve. The French Commander-in-Chief received orders directly from Napoleon to make sail for Naples. But to do so at that time, would have been negligent, or so the French Admiral thought. He decided that the best way to avoid Nelson's blockade, was to wait for a favourable wind, and then make a run for it, so he intended to do just that. However, after another two days of waiting inside the safety of Cadiz harbour, Villeneuve changed his mind and decided to make sail immediately.

It was ironic that he'd already recognised Napoleon's orders were impossible to execute, and that his Emperor was lacking in the concept of naval warfare. Villeneuve was also aware that, in the belief that his commander in charge of the combined fleet was a coward, Napoleon was sending his replacement. It was that knowledge, which rankled with the French Admiral, and rather than be branded a coward, decided to make his move, even if it resulted in his death, which was preferable to being labelled as being cowardly.

It was HMS Mars that first signalled to the flagship that the enemy was coming out of port.

Midshipman Pollard first sighted the signal and hurriedly informed Nelson.

The Vice Admiral banged his desk with his fist, and declared, "At last, finally our time has come." He then instructed Pollard to signal back, 'from flag to Mars, current bearing?'.

The reply came instantly back, 'South East'.

Pollard read the look of excitement on Nelson's face. His chain of communication had worked successfully. His frigates had seen Villeneuve leave Cadiz and the signal had got back to him quickly. Now, it was imperative that the British moved with all haste. Nelson had to ensure the French weren't able to reach the open Atlantic, as they had done so previously, or retreat to the eastwards and Toulon. Also, there was a need to cut off any attempt to escape back into Cadiz.

The chase was on, and the fastest ships in the British fleet were instructed to go ahead during the night, carrying lights.

"Shall I clear for action sir?" Captain Hardy enquired of his Admiral.

"No, not yet Hardy. Let us first see what our Parisienne mouse intends to do."

Once again, Nelson called for his Signal Midshipman, and ordered John Pollard to signal both HMS Britannia Prince and HMS Dreadnought, both being heavy sailors, 'to take stations as convenient'. The signals continued being received from the two pursuing ships, which kept the French in sight throughout that night. Very few men got any sleep during that activity, and as the grey of dawn approached, the British found themselves standing towards an enemy fleet, that was finally manoeuvring to meet them.

When realising a confrontation was imminent, Pollard and Smiley glanced at each other, without speaking a word. All the past training and experience of every member of the crew had been for this very moment. The orders to the men continued to be shouted out by Captain Hardy and his lieutenants, as the British fleet now began to create the two columns, which were a fundamental part of their Commander-in-Chiefs plan.

Villeneuve's experience at the Battle of the Nile helped him to guess what Nelson's attack plan was likely to be, so gave orders to his captains to perform in the same manner. In other words, to act on their own initiative, ensuring they were always beside an enemy ship. The problem the French Admiral faced though was, whereby Nelson had spent months preparing his captains in readiness to use the tactics of his plan, the French and Spanish had remained in favour of using the more conventional idea of parallel lines of battle. Therefore, Villeneuve was faced with the only option of forming the line he knew Nelson would be expecting.

There was a heavy swell, but little wind, as the enemy attempted to move into a singular line made up of three divisions. Their manoeuvring into position was slow and awkward, and the French Admiral could only watch from his flagship, the two columns of British ships moving sedately but purposefully towards his disorganised line.

The same lack of wind, which was hampering the enemy ships, also resulted in the British fleet approaching painfully slowly.

"Now, you may clear for action Mr. Hardy," Nelson ordered.

Each ship became a hive of activity. Powder cartridges were brought to the guns, together with buckets of water, as the drums rolled and the men moved into their positions. The decks were sanded and the guns loaded before being run out, with the gunners stood in readiness to fire, holding slow burn matches away from the powder cartridges.

Midshipman Smiley assisted the First Lieutenant in organising the gun crews on the upper decks, whilst the second and third lieutenants supervised the same on the lower decks.

Midshipman Pollard remained close to Nelson, in readiness for sending more signals. But the Commander-in-Chief returned to his cabin, instructing the marine outside his door to allow no other person access. With the ship being cleared for action, the inside of his stronghold had already had the furniture removed. He therefore knelt on the floor, and found time to write his last diary entry. It read as follows:

'At day light saw the enemy's combined fleet from East to East South East bore away and made the signal to order of sailing and to prepare for battle with the enemy with their heads to Southward, at seven the enemy wearing in succession. May the Great God whom I worship, grant to my country and for the benefit of Europe in general, a great and glorious victory, and may no misconduct in any one tarnish it, and may humanity after victory, be the predominant feature in the British fleet, for myself individually I commit my life to Him who made me, and may His blessing light upon my endeavours for serving my country faithfully. To Him I resign myself and the just cause which is entrusted to me to defend. Amen, Amen, Amen'.

As the British fleet sailed closer to the enemy, Nelson counted forty ships, thirty-four of which were ships of the line and six frigates, but they were still some distance away. It was then that the Neptune tried to overtake Victory, which was leading one of the two columns, the other being led by Vice Admiral Collingwood. Nelson immediately ordered the Neptune's captain, Thomas Fremantle, to drop back, having acknowledged the man was only attempting to take the enemy flack away from his commanding officer.

It took hours to reach the enemy's position, owing to the lack of wind, and it could be seen that the combined enemy fleet had formed an arc, with the middle ships pushed further back to make it more difficult for the British ships to breach the line. It was time for Nelson to send a signal to the fleet which was eventually given a place in Britain's history of sea warfare. Initially, he wanted the signal to declare, 'England confides that every man will do his duty.'

Midshipman Pollard acknowledged the instruction, but when he attempted to send the signal, he found that the word 'confides' was not included in the signal vocabulary, and reported the problem to the First Lieutenant. When it was suggested to Nelson that the awkward word should be replaced by, 'expects', the Commander-in-Chief impatiently agreed, wanting to send another signal before he ran out of time. Hence the signal sent to the fleet read, 'England expects that every man will do his duty'.

The signal was met with cheers from every ship in the fleet. Nelson's men were aware of his affection for them, and the trust he gave to them. The battle just off Trafalgar, which would forever earn its place in history, was about to commence with the British crews in good heart, and a determination to achieve victory for their Commander-in-Chief.

Chapter Seventeen

As the British fleet drew closer to the enemy lines, Nelson was anxious to send one more signal to his captains. It was to 'engage more closely', and the Signal Midshipman was instructed to leave the same message flying throughout the ensuing battle, which John Pollard did.

Close action was Nelson's preferred method of battle, having been successfully deployed at the battles of the Nile and Copenhagen. In this instance, he knew that such a tactic would create confusion, taking notice that the enemy line had been divided into three parts. There certainly would not be any further opportunity to send signals, and each captain had been instructed to find his own target. His intention was to completely confound the French and Spanish. The greater the confusion the weaker they would become.

Vice Admiral Collingwood in his flagship, the Royal Sovereign, headed the first column towards the enemy line, and as soon as he came within range of their guns, the battle commenced. Broadsides were fired from several opposing ships, battering the British leading vessel. During what could only be described as a perilous ten-minute period, Collingwood's gunners were unable to respond with his penetrating British ships running directly towards the enemy lines with their bows first. Although such a head-on manoeuvre helped make the vessels smaller targets, it was disturbing and perilous to face so much hostile action without being able to return fire. Just as Nelson had anticipated, fortunately for the men aboard the Royal Sovereign, the Spanish and French gunners were incompetent compared with their counterparts, and failed miserably in their attempt to destroy Collingwood's flag ship. Again, it was a factor the Commander-in-Chief had been gambling on.

Finally, Collingwood managed to break the enemy's line by sailing between the Spanish ship, 'Santa Ana' and the French, 'Fougueux', both ships disorganised and leaving a gap in the enemy line. The order to return fire was given at last, and many of the Spanish ship's crew were killed or wounded, as the British ship continued to target the Santa Ana's stern, as she broke through the line. The Royal Sovereign then closed in on the Spanish vessel, almost touching her side with her cannon. That part of the British ploy was being enacted successfully.

As she raked the Santa Ana's decks, the enemy were quick to respond and the Royal Sovereign soon found herself surrounded by the Fougueux, Indomptable, and two other Spanish ships. The Belleisle, which was part of

Collingwood's column came to her assistance, losing as many as fifty men during her approach. She became engaged with the Fougueux and the two ships were locked together, like two gladiators gripped in mortal combat.

The Mars was next to breach the enemy line and fired at point blank range at the French ship of war, Pluton, resulting in devastating damage and loss of life. Other British ships descended down on the gaps now being left in the enemy line, and the battle was already turning towards chaos, with the combined fleet broken and confused.

Just as Nelson had hoped for, in the general melee, the British ships pulled alongside the French and Spanish, continuing to inflict their wrath upon the enemy, with gunners constantly firing and reloading under the shouts from their supervising officers. There was pandemonium on the vessels from both sides of the engagement, and a smoke screen, which had formed around those ships attacking and defending, made it difficult to see from a distance, how the battle was actually progressing, or otherwise.

One of the French ships. The Monarca, lost six hundred men killed or wounded, but was offered no respite as she was made to suffer more under the guns of HMS Bellerophon.

Other breaks in the enemy line became apparent, and battles continued to be raged between individual ships. Nelson had been watching closely how Collingwood and his column of ships were faring, and when he thought the time was right, led his own column on a course away from

Villeneuve's flagship, towards a point further down the line. The French commander had not been looking forward to a one-on-one confrontation with the Victory, and felt some relief when he observed Nelson's flagship moving away from his own position. That relief was short lived though. The British Commander-in-Chiefs manoeuvre was a ruse, and the French Admiral was surprised when Nelson suddenly turned Victory's bow back, bearing down on Villeneuve's flagship, the Bucentaure.

Half an hour after Collingwood in the Royal Sovereign had broken through the enemy line, Nelson arrived in HMS Victory, and managed to attack Villeneuve's flagship. However, the assault was quickly impeded by telling damage from the guns of the French Heros, the Spanish Santisima Trinidad, and the Bucentaure. Victory's wheel had disappeared, and Hardy was forced to immediately send one of his lieutenants below deck with forty men to use the tiller. The two midshipmen, Smiley and Pollard were then instructed to convey instructions to the working party by physically running down to them. Both junior officers would then return to the upper decks to receive further instructions for communicating to the work detail.

Rails exploded, sending large splinters of wood across Victory's decks, as enemy fire found their targets. The quarterdeck in particular, became saturated in blood, with men and officers being killed or severely wounded. Casualties were carried as best as possible down below decks to the surgeon, who was having his own personal nightmare in attempting to treat the wounded quickly. Choking black smoke covered the whole ship, as the guns continued to fire, but the incoming shot was crippling Victory and striking home far too readily, as her crew continued working in what could only be described as a dense fog.

Nelson's continued presence on the quarterdeck of Victory, was a typical gesture by the Commander-in-Chief, and as if challenging the French to pick him out, he wore his bright uniform with his four stars stitched across his chest. Such daring behaviour undoubtedly raised his crews' morale even further, although he made himself a sitting target for the French snipers. Midshipman Pollard was concerned about the Admiral displaying himself in such a flashy manner, as were other officers, but they had not the courage to suggest their leader dressed down, or even retired to the safety of his cabin. Such a suggestion would have been the ultimate insult to a man who seemed to be facing the surrounding dangers with impunity, apparently in the belief he was invulnerable against any enemy fire.

Still the cannons continued to roar out, rocking the Victory from side to side with their heavy recoils. Officers continued screaming out their orders and doing all in their power to direct and motivate their men. Marines fired their muskets at surrounding enemy ships, aiming high to pick off snipers perched in the rigging of the French and Spanish ships. What fires suddenly ignited, were quickly doused and all the training and rehearsals undertaken whilst at sea, were stretched to the very limit.

Victory had made a slow and steady approach to the area of hostility, with Nelson conspicuously patrolling her gundecks, giving rousing speeches and rallying his men, who were inspired by his presence. He then returned to the quarterdeck and paced up and down with Captain Hardy and his secretary, John Scott at his side.

Before the flagship had been sufficiently close enough to open fire on the enemy, she sustained more damage, and losses to her crew were mounting up. One single shot managed to kill eight marines, and Nelson immediately ordered Captain Adair to spread his red coated men about the ship more. But the reality of the battle struck home to the Vice Admiral, when his secretary was unexpectedly cut in half by a cannon ball. After Scott's body had been thrown overboard, Nelson noticed his stockings were saturated with his former secretary's blood, but obstinately remained in full sight of the French on the quarterdeck.

Another shot from the enemy, brought more realisation of the peril Nelson was facing. The ball ploughed into the deck between the Admiral and his captain, sending a splinter of wood flying and breaking the buckle on Hardy's shoe. Midshipman Pollard, who was standing nearby, waiting for further instructions to deliver to those working the tiller below deck, overheard Nelson say, "This is too warm work, Hardy, to last long."

"Yes, My Lord."

Victory's crew were being tested to the limit. Four enemy ships had thrown all they had at them, at a time when they were under orders not to reply. Nelson commented that he had never before seen so much courage, as he did with those men during Victory's approach towards the enemy line.

The French Commander-in-Chief, Admiral Villeneuve, watched with trepidation from the quarterdeck of his flagship, Bucentaure, Nelson's approach in Victory. He feared that the British commander was heading either for his ship, or for the Santisima Trinidad. Villeneuve's immediate problem was that the five ships in his vanguard, under Rear Admiral Dumanoir, were a fair distance away from his position and assistance would be doubtful. By the time those ships turned about, it would be too late. And that was what Nelson's plan was all about. Such a situation was exactly what he had been praying for.

Villeneuve immediately signalled for any ship not engaged, to join the action instantly. It was obvious that the French Admiral required Dumanoir to retreat back and enter the action close to the Bucentaure. However, whether the captain thought the signal was not for his attention, or could not see it through the thick smoke and distance, he failed to return and assist his Commander-in-Chief.

Nelson had succeeded in cutting off the vanguard and making them impotent, knowing it would take time for the other ships of the line to turn around and return to assist their flagship. The longer it took them, the better for Nelson, giving him some parity in numbers.

It was at that stage of the battle, the Bicemtaire, the Santisima Trinidad and the Redoutable, managed to close the gaps between them. Having been denied the opportunity to fulfil that part of his plan, to get behind the enemy line with his column, any other Admiral would have undoubtedly chosen to turn and run alongside the enemy ships, resorting to traditional tactics. But not Nelson. He ordered Hardy to ram one of the ships to move it out of the way, and create an opening in the enemy line. When asked which one, he told his captain it would make no difference, as long as he could get his column to the back of the opposing ships. It therefore transpired that Hardy rammed the Redoutable, at the same time firing at Bucentaure's stern.

Both Victory and Redoutable locked together with their rigging becoming entangled with each other.

Captain Eliab Harvey's HMS Temeraire was a ninety-eight-gun powerhouse, which came forth through the smoke, firing at those ships close to Victory and gaining a position where she could fire broadsides into the Redoutable. A general melee was now forming around Villeneuve's flagship Bucentaure, which was totally covered in the same clouds of black smoke, resulting from the firing of cannons from both sides of the conflict. Years of confrontation were being played out unmercifully, with each opposing side determined to annihilate the other.

One other British ship joined that part of the battle, having already fought her way through the French and Spanish defences. During the night before the battle, the small 64-gun ship, HMS Africa, had been positioned far to the north of the rest of the British fleet. Nelson had signalled her captain, Henry Digby, to 'make all sail', meaning for the vessel to speed away from the battle. Digby, being an obstinate individual chose to misread the signal, interpreting it as meaning his ship should sail with all haste towards the remainder of the British fleet.

At that time, there were no fewer than ten enemy vessels between the Africa and Nelson's position, the majority being much bigger with a greater compliment of guns than Digby's vessel. Amazingly, the small British war ship weaved her way through the line, firing at each of Dumanoir's ships with both broadsides. When she arrived at the ongoing confrontation close to the Victory, Captain Digby had the nerve and audacity to pull alongside the Spanish giant, Santisma Trinidad, and ignoring her one hundred and thirty guns, opened fire on her. Digby then sent a party over to board the Spanish vessel, but they were soon sent packing by the Santisma Trinidad's commander.

The Africa then turned her guns on the French warship, Intrepide and a battle pursued between the two ships for forty minutes, until other British ships arrived and forced the Intrepide to surrender. But by this time, the ferocity of the ongoing battle between Victory and Redoutable was intense and deadly.

Redoutable's hull had been destroyed, and almost every man on her lower decks was injured or dead. Her gun ports were closed, to prevent the British from boarding her through those openings, but above decks, and from the rigging, musketeers were raining down bullets upon Victory's crew. Redoutable's Captain Lucas boasted he had the best and most highly trained musketeers in France, and their objective was to put down any attempt to deploy boarders from Victory's decks.

Midshipman Pollard stood at the side of his friend, Smiley, still mesmerised by the manner in which Nelson continued to pace the quarterdeck with Captain Hardy at his side. Victory's position at that moment wasn't good. Despite the forty men working hard on the tiller below decks, she had sustained heavy damage and remained virtually immoveable. Pollard pointed out the French snipers clinging to the rigging above their heads to Midshipman Smiley, and both grabbed muskets and ammunition pouches, once belonging to fallen marines. They began to return fire, bringing down at least some of the enemy snipers. Still, the lead balls continued to rain down, ploughing into the wooden decks, and Midshipman Smiley was trying to shout out something, but was inaudible owing to the noise of battle that was ongoing around them.

As Nelson's men continued to resist the enemy onslaught by fighting would-be boarders from Redoutable hand to hand, red coated marines and crewmen became entangled with pistols and cutlasses, amongst the French intruders. Utter carnage was surrounding each of Victory's severely damaged masts, beneath a blackened sky.

Suddenly, as though he was back reliving the same dream, he had experienced so many years previously, Pollard watched as a musketeer drew a bead on Nelson. He cried out to no one in particular, fighting hard to reload his musket, but couldn't act quickly enough to avoid the inevitable. He screamed across at Smiley to bear his musket in the direction of the single sniper poised to take his shot from the rigging above their heads, but his words of warning failed to penetrate the noise surrounding them.

Mere seconds separated the two hostile acts. The musketeer fired, before Pollard aimed and returned fire, causing the sniper to fall from the rigging on to the deck below. The young midshipman knew instantly what had happened, and when he looked through the smoke, towards where he had last seen Nelson standing, saw his prone body lying on the deck with Captain Hardy crouching down beside him with another lieutenant. The Vice Admiral's hat was missing and he was being propped up by his flag captain, the bright front of his tunic covered in blood.

Without hesitation, Pollard ran to where the Commander-in-Chief was lying, mortally wounded, and Hardy immediately ordered him to fetch some sacking from down below.

"And be quick about it," was the loud and distressed instruction given.

Before the young man from Plymouth left, he heard Nelson gasp, "They have done for me at last...my backbone is shot through."

The fierceness of the battle continued, with more blood being shed; more bodies falling, and more screams filling the air. Men were fighting in hand to hand combat, and it was looking highly unlikely that HMS Victory was going to survive the day.

Chapter Eighteen

Nelson had fallen in exactly the same spot where his secretary, John Scott, had earlier been killed. The Vice Admiral's ashen face looked all around him, as he attempted to initially support himself with his one arm, until that buckled beneath him. Thomas Hardy never left his side, as the battle raged on and the defenders of Victory continued in a courageous bid to fend off the would-be French boarders. By the time Midshipman Pollard had returned with a hessian sack, the stricken Nelson was being propped up by the captain and three other seamen. He was in obvious shock and his glazed eyes were looking but not really seeing. The deck beneath where he so helplessly lay was covered in his blood.

It was Hardy who placed the sacking over Nelson's face and bloodstained torso, before lifting him from the deck. It was a vain attempt to conceal the Admiral from his men, before instructing those in attendance to carry their wounded leader down to where the surgeon, Beatty, was operating. They wasted little time and Nelson was hurriedly transferred down into what was an extremely dark and grim scene.

There was only one flickering light above the surgeon's table, which contained his instruments, most of which resembled a butcher's tools. There was blood everywhere with buckets containing amputated limbs littering the wooden floor. The stench of death was prolific, and men lay prostrate close by; some groaning; others screaming. There was no pain relief available, only a strip of leather for victims of the ongoing battle to bite on, when Beatty did his painful but necessary work.

Nelson was taken to an area where he would not be seen by any of the wounded and dying, stripped of his clothing and covered with a blanket. He was then propped up, and the Reverend Scott, who had been handing out lemonade to the injured in an effort to offer them some kind of comfort, appeared at the Admiral's side. When the Commander-in-Chief opened his eyes, he addressed the man of the cloth, mistaking him for the surgeon.

"Doctor, I told you so; Doctor, I am gone!" He then quietly added, "I have to leave Lady Hamilton and my adopted daughter Horatia, as a legacy to my country." Frothy blood was visible coming from his mouth.

Beatty then appeared and examined him. Nelson told the ship's doctor he had no feeling in his legs and was aware his spine was broken. He was having difficulty in breathing, and every minute, could feel a gush in his chest. The musket ball had entered through Nelson's shoulder and broken his collar bone, before travelling diagonally downwards and piercing his pulmonary artery in his lungs. His chest cavity was slowly filling with blood and after fracturing a vertebra, had finally come to rest in his spine. There was no exit wound, which told the surgeon, the devastating lead ball was still inside his upper body.

Tears filled the eyes of those gathered around their fallen leader, whilst others prayed quietly for his salvation. But they all knew their Commander-in-Chief had fought his last battle and was in fact, in the grip of death.

"You can do nothing for me," he told Beatty, "I have but a short time to live; my back is shot through." He insisted the surgeon attended others, rather than waste time trying to tend to his wounds, which was a helpless task.

The sound of the ongoing fierce battle above, could still be heard, occasionally attracting Nelson's attention. Even as he lay there, dying, the Vice Admiral gave orders for Hardy to return to the upper decks and continue to play his role in the battle. The captain obeyed, taking Midshipman Pollard with him, and determined to bring news back to Nelson of another victory.

When they reached the quarter deck, Hardy turned to Pollard and declared, "I saw what you did," obviously referring to the Plymouth man having brought down the French musketeer responsible for wounding

Nelson, "And can assure you, the appropriate thanks will be accredited to you."

"I would rather that His Lordship lived sir," Pollard answered with sincerity.

Hardy nodded, and the young Midshipman was instantly, emotionally disturbed when seeing tears trickling down the captain's blackened face.

The turmoil was continuing, and it appeared the Victory was on the very brink of defeat, as marauding sailors and officers from the Redoutable were fighting like mad dogs to board Nelson's flag ship. Both the captain and midshipman joined in the melee, waving and thrusting cutlasses and daggers, helping to repel the enemy invasion of Victory.

Captain Eliab Harvey's HMS Temeraire, quickly saw that HMS Victory was about to be overrun, and began to fire broadsides at the Redoutable, killing and wounding many of its remaining crew. It was an unexpected onslaught that took the enemy by surprise. The French boarding crews were called back to defend Redoutable from the jaws of defeat, being subjected to countless broadsides by the Temeraire, until she had virtually been eliminated from the battle. Finally, she surrendered to Victory and Nelson's flagship was saved.

Admiral Villeneuve again sent a signal to Dumanoir, ordering him to return, but received no signal in reply. He was aware his ship, Bucentaure, could not take much further punishment, so, finally struck his colours, surrendering to HMS Conqueror. As soon as the French saw that their Commander-in-Chief had capitulated, their morale nose-dived, and both Spanish and French ships began to lower their flags in clusters, as the British continued to bombard them with cannon fire. The task of annihilating the combined fleets of the enemy had to be concluded successfully. There could be no possibility of another battle of such ferocity as that being fought at Trafalgar, being ever repeated in the future. The cost in human life was far too high.

Midshipman Pollard was looking for his friend and colleague, Arthur Smiley, as the other members of the crew cheered boisterously each time an enemy ship struck its colours. Eventually, he found the other young midshipman lying on the deck, beneath another seaman's body. His face was as white as snow and his chest was saturated with blood. Pollard crouched down and placed an arm around Smiley's shoulder, lifting him from the deck, but it was too late. His friend was dead, killed by a musket ball penetrating through his chest. It was a devastating experience for the young man from Plymouth, and although he kept repeating his name, there was no response. There was to be no engagement to Rose; no peals of wedding bells echoing around Plymouth Sound to celebrate the happy couple. In fact, there would never be any response from his closest friend, ever again.

One of the older members of the crew placed a hand on the tearful midshipman's shoulder and explained, "He fought like a hero sir. He killed three of them, before they finally saw to him."

Pollard looked up at the old seadog, who from his lined and ashen face, appeared to have been one of the many brave defenders who had stopped the French boarders, before victory had been achieved.

"Thank you," he whispered, with tears cascading down both sides of his ashen face.

Just over one hour after Nelson had been wounded, Captain Hardy returned to his fallen commander's side. They shook hands affectionately and His Lordship enquired in a weak voice, "Well Hardy, how goes the battle? How goes the day with us?"

"Very well my Lord," Hardy answered, with confidence, trying hard to conceal his personal grief, "You have a victory."

"I am a dead man Hardy. I am going fast," Nelson whispered to his flag captain, "Come nearer to me. Pray let my dear Lady Hamilton have my hair, and all other things belonging to me."

Hardy told him that he hoped Mr. Beatty could yet hold out some prospect of life, but Nelson rejected the suggestion.

"Oh no," he answered, "It is impossible. My back is shot through. Beatty will tell you so."

Captain Hardy's grief was beginning to overwhelm him. The sight of his revered friend and commander slowly succumbing to death was too much to bear, and he returned back to the upper decks. But before parting for the last time, both men shook hands again, with Nelson barely having the strength to grip his flag captain's hand. Just fifteen minutes following Hardy's departure, Nelson became speechless, and his steward found the surgeon to express his apprehension that the Admiral was nearing the end of his life.

Beatty once again attended Nelson, to find he was on the verge of dissolution. He knelt down by his side and took up his hand, which was cold. The pulse in his wrist had gone and his forehead also felt like ice. Five minutes after that examination, Beatty witnessed Nelson take his last dying breath.

Up above, the noise of battle had subsided, as Britain claimed victory over the French and Spanish, bringing to a conclusive end the possibility of Napoleon ever landing his troops on the shores of England, his navy having been all but destroyed.

A devastated Midshipman Pollard had witnessed the deaths of his closest friend and that of a man who had been an icon to him throughout most of his young life, and both on the same day. He stood staring at nothing in particular, on the quarterdeck, dejected and exhausted. The victory had been made bitter sweet with the loss of the man who had planned the defeat of Britain's principle enemies. But for the young man from Plymouth, his grief had been enlarged ten-fold by the knowledge he would never again enter into conversation with his dearest friend and colleague, Midshipman Smiley.

"We paid a heavy price for our achievements this day lad," a voice spoke from behind him. It was Captain Hardy, looking like a man who had been torn apart, rather than a victor of one of the most ferocious sea battles ever fought.

"Yes sir, the heaviest I fear," Pollard whispered in reply.

The captain placed a hand on the young man's shoulder, in similar fashion to how Thomas Pollard would have done if he had been alive and there at his son's elbow. After a pause of a few seconds, Hardy then instructed the midshipman to secure Nelson's cabin, and relay his orders to the sentry that no one was to be allowed entry.

Pollard nodded, and with both shoulders slumped, as though he was carrying the problems of the world on his back, slowly made his way beneath the poop deck, towards the armed marine still standing guard outside the Vice Admiral's door.

Once inside the small cabin, the young officer stood for a few moments, still trying to come to terms with Midshipman Smiley's death. A thousand thoughts swamped his mind, yet not one made any sense. He appreciated the battle had been necessary to save England from invasion, but at what price? So many dead; so many maimed and disabled; so many never to again live their lives as they had in the past. So many sacrifices made, including the life of his friend, and that of Nelson himself. Just how dominant the Royal Navy would be without the presence of the most famous sailor of them all, was a thought that he allowed to remain for a split second. It was a question to be answered by other more educated men than himself, and should be of no concern to his own intellectual abilities.

As he was about to turn and convey to the sentry outside, Captain Hardy's orders, he noticed what looked like an open letter resting on the floor. There was a pen and bottle of ink at one side. Pollard crouched down and recovered the item, immediately recognising it had been written in Nelson's hand and was addressed to Lady Hamilton.

His tears began to fall, as he read with difficulty the handwritten words:

'Victory, October 19th 1805, Noon, Cadiz, E.S.E., 16 Leagues.

My dearest beloved Emma, the dear friend of my bosom. The signal has been made that the enemy's combined fleet are coming out of port. We have very little wind, so that I have no hopes of seeing them before tomorrow. May the God of Battles crown my endeavours with success; at all events, I will take care that my name shall ever be most dear to you and Horatia, both of whom I love as much as my own life. And as my last writing before the battle will be to you, so I hope in God that I shall live to finish my letter after the battle. May Heaven bless you prays your...'

It was the very last thing Nelson had written and at first, Pollard was undecided as to what to do with it. Of course, it would be required to be delivered to the lady to whom it was addressed, but that shouldn't be his duty. How could it possibly be? The lady in question moved in far higher social circles than John Pollard could even imagine in his wildest dreams. With extreme care, the midshipman folded the paper and placed it inside his tunic. When he returned to the upper deck, he sought out Captain Hardy, who was standing on the quarterdeck in conversation with Captain Eliab Harvey from the Temeraire. Both men appeared to be in mourning and young Pollard immediately handed the personal letter to his captain.

After reading it, Hardy nodded and swore to see to its safe delivery to Lady Hamilton.

"Leave it with me Mr. Pollard," he said, "And I am sorry about the loss of your friend Mr. Smiley. He was an excellent and brave young officer."

"Aye sir, that he was sir."

The Battle of Trafalgar had taken place in the Atlantic Ocean off the southwest coast of Spain, and just west of Cape Trafalgar, near the town of Los Canos de Meca. Twenty-seven British ships of the line led by Admiral Lord Nelson aboard HMS Victory defeated thirty-three French and Spanish ships of the line under French Admiral Villeneuve. The Franco-Spanish fleet lost twenty-two ships. The British lost none.

HMS Victory was severely damaged during the battle and was unable to move under her own sail. HMS Neptune was tasked with towing her to

Gibraltar for repairs. She then sailed with Nelson's body to England, where, after lying in state at Greenwich, he was buried in St Paul's Cathedral on 9 January 1806. The whole British nation mourned the loss of their favourite son.

After Trafalgar, John Pollard was promoted to lieutenant, serving in HMS Queen off Cadiz. He also served in HMS Dreadnought and HMS Hibernian. Lieutenant Pollard's final active service was in HMS Kattegat at Brunswick.

He spent fourteen years on half pay, during which time in 1822, he married and eventually had six children, before being given a post in the reserve at Chatham for three years. From 1836, John Pollard served in the coastguard in Ireland. In 1853, he was finally appointed a lieutenant of Greenwich Hospital and later made an honorary retired commander in recognition of having been the man who had avenged Lord Nelson at Trafalgar.

His sister, Rose Pollard, became a successful retail business lady, working in the dress making industry, and also later married and had a number of children. Both Rose and her brother never forgot the midshipman with one arm, Arthur Smiley.

Some 63 years after the Battle of Trafalgar, John Pollard died in the Greenwich Hospital on 22 April 1868, to be widely recognised forever, as the man who had avenged Nelson.

About the Author

John Plimmer was a high-profile Detective Superintendent with West Midlands Police during which time he investigated over thirty murders, all of which were detected. He studied Law and Philosophy at Birmingham University and has been a feature writer for both the Sunday Mercury and Evening Mail newspapers. Plimmer has also written numerous articles published in various magazines, and has been involved in script writing for some of television's most popular dramas.

He is a prolific novelist and to date has over forty books published. Some of his works include 'Brickbats and Tutus' - the biography of Julie Felix, Britain's first black ballerina, and Backstreet Urchins – a humorous account of life in the Birmingham slums of post war Britain.

The eight book 'Dan Mitchell' series involves international espionage and murder, and his popular Victorian Detective Casebook series includes thirteen books describing the adventures of Richard Rayner and Henry Bustle of Scotland Yard.

Other published books in the Victorian Casebook series:

Printed in Great Britain
by Amazon

42478777R00151